# A
# Love
# of Time

## David L. Gurnee

D0839128

*To Paul
and Sherry,
There is
a love!
9/3/01*

*Mack City*

# A Love of Time
by David L. Gurnee
©2001 David L. Gurnee

Music: *For Kathleen*
by David L. Gurnee
©2001 David L. Gurnee

This story is a work of fiction. Characters and incidents are fictitious, and are products of the author's imagination.

All rights reserved. No part of this book may be reproduced or utilized in any form or by any means, electronic or mechanical, including photocopying, recording, or by any information storage or retrieval system, without permission in writing from the publisher.

Printed in the United States of America by:

**WindTime Publications**
**Box 1934**
**Mackinac Island, MI 49757**
**www.windtime.com**

First Printing: July 2001

Works by David L. Gurnee:

Books:
*Memoirs of Elise*
*A Love of Time*
*Collaboration*
*Add Cinema and Stir*

Music CDs:
*The Winds of Time*
*Coming Home*
*Themes*

## Acknowledgments

Thanks and love to my wife and daughter who have constantly encouraged me. Thanks to all our wonderful friends who have been so very supportive. This is *real* fun.

# For Kathleen

# Journey
# to
# Paradise

ONE

# Till the Lilacs Bloom

It was the summer of 1975, and it was my first and last time on Mackinac Island. Her name was Kathleen, and I loved her more than life itself.

\*     \*     \*

I had always wanted to visit Mackinac Island, ever since I was seven years old, and my mother took me to the movies to see *This Time for Keeps*. I was so impressed by Mackinac's deep blue waters, the big boats pulling into the harbor, the beautiful mansions on the bluffs, and the turn of the century look of the island. But most of all, I was impressed by the hundreds of lilacs that covered the island.

When I was growing up in Kansas, we had a single lilac bush in our back yard. I would sit next to it for hours, inhaling and being overwhelmed by its fragrance. I was absolutely convinced that this fragrance was proof of the existence of God; proof of the romance between Creator and creation. So when I saw the part in *This Time for Keeps* that showed the lilacs that covered the island, and heard the musical accompaniment, *when it's lilac time on Mackinac*, I was convinced that Mackinac Island must be paradise.

As I crossed the Mackinac Bridge that day in mid-May, 1975, I could see Mackinac Island in the distance, its white buildings gleaming in the sun. I thought of how strange the circumstances were that had finally brought me here to paradise.

My father left my mother and me when I was four years old. He just left, went to a ball game, and never came back. My mother believed that foul play (no pun intended) was involved, and that somehow, my father had met his end. When she died in 1972, she still believed that. Then I received a phone call from an attorney in the fall of 1974. My father had died that September, and he had left me everything he owned: close to three million dollars, a large house in Ohio, and an island in the upper peninsula of Michigan — a small island in a chain of islands called Les Cheneaux.

Learning that my father had been alive all those years and had allowed my mother and me to think he was dead, affected me deeply. At first I was angry with my father, because I felt that he had deliberately abandoned us. But then I found out that, though he had remarried, he had never had any other children. And then, for some reason, I became angry with my mother, thinking that *she* must have done something to drive him away. I shuffled through myriad reasons to understand what he had done, and why he had done it. But, eventually, the only reason my mind would accept was this: he was simply unhappy. Maybe my mind accepted this reason, because of my own situation.

I'd spent most of my life waiting for the woman of my dreams. I didn't care how long I had to wait. I just wanted the whole enchilada. Till death do us part. The whole works. But somewhere along the line I just gave up. I got tired of waiting. And that was when I met Julie.

Julie was tired of waiting too. We really weren't *right* for each other, but we were *there* for each other. My mom had just died. Julie was going through tough times. It was just timing.

Julie was a great person, with a wonderful daughter, Anna. We lived together for several years, but we never really made the connection as people. We were just too different. I had wanted to end the relationship for quite some time, and I was sure Julie felt the same way. But it was never convenient to end it. We both looked out for each other financially. When Julie was down on funds, *I* always seemed to have money, and when *I* was down, *she* always seemed to have money. It just wasn't convenient financially to make the split.

But most of all, we cared about Anna. Anna's father had cut out on them right after Anna was born. Julie knew Anna needed a father, and I didn't want Anna to grow up the way I had, without a father. But when the inheritance came, I couldn't justify the relationship any longer. I gave Julie $500,000, and put another $500,000 in a trust fund for Anna. Julie and I broke up, and I moved out on my own.

Some say that money changes people, but I don't entirely believe that. I think it just changes circumstances. People are basically just as selfish or benevolent as they were before they had the money, except now they have the means to be more selfish, or more giving. Money seems to bring things to the surface.

A few of our "friends" thought I had done a horrible thing; thought that the money had gone to my head, and that the money I gave to Julie was just to ease my own conscience. But Julie and I both knew the motives, and neither of us felt compelled to explain it to anyone. As they say: *Your friends don't need an explanation, and your enemies wouldn't believe it anyway.*

Having the money helped Julie and me to do something that was long overdue — to get honest about our relationship and to do something about it. Julie would have to find someone she really cared about, and someone that would be a good father to Anna. I would have to stop pretending that I was happy, and make some changes in my life. The money helped facilitate that. And as far as the *amount* that I gave to Julie; I felt that I owed her a lot more.

Three million might sound like a lot of money, but once Uncle Sam got through with it, and after the lawyers got through with *me*, there wasn't much left. I sold my father's house to help pay for taxes and legal expenses. And when the dust cleared, I had my personal belongings, a Mercedes, $500,000 in the bank, and an island in Michigan.

And that's why I decided to take the trip to Michigan that May. To see my island. I thought that if the island was suitable, that maybe I would build a cabin on it, and hibernate there for the rest of my life. But a sign changed my life. The rest of my life.

As I headed north on I-75 near the Mackinac Bridge, I saw the sign: *VISIT BEAUTIFUL MACKINAC ISLAND*. I don't know where I thought Mackinac Island was. I guess as a child I thought it was on the ocean, because of the big ships that I saw in *This Time for Keeps*. I just hadn't put it all together; that Mackinac Island was in the U.P. of Michigan. All my life I had dreamed of visiting Mackinac Island, and I knew I had to go there, if only for a few hours.

Pulling into St. Ignace that mid-May afternoon, was like pulling into a New England fishing village. The shore was lined with docks, and small fishing boats, and nets, and fishermen selling their catch right off the docks. The only sign of tourism was the occasional moccasin and tomahawk shop, and the ferry line billboards competing for your business to the island, using language that led you to believe that their line was the *only* way to get to the island, or the fastest way, or at the very least, the *safest* way.

I pulled into the ferry dock at about five minutes till two, and just barely made it in time to catch the ferry. I quickly parked my car, gave my keys and bags to the attendant, and then walked toward the boat. I looked up at the bright green letters painted on the port side of the boat: *Huron*. I paused for a moment, and then crossed the ramp onto the boat.

"Right up the stairs to the upper level," one of the deck-hands said to me, and he pointed toward one of the two narrow stairways near the back of the boat.

Behind me, I heard a cart being wheeled onto the boat, and then the harsh sound of the metal ramp being pulled across the metal deck, onto the boat. I felt the boat moving away from the dock, as I ascended the stairs, trying to keep my balance. When I got to the top of the stairs, I went straight to the back of the boat. I looked down into the crystal blue water, and even though the boat's propeller was churning up the water, I could still see the bottom of the lake.

The boat pulled out of the harbor, and began to undulate slowly over the waves, moving toward the island. The slow rocking of the boat felt like the gentle rhythm of an adagio, and I began to hear a melody in my mind.

I'd been a newspaper reporter for nearly ten years, and the history of the newspaper business fascinated me. In high school, courses on typesetting were required vocational training, even though manual typesetting hadn't been used for years. I'd done some work with old plate photography: gunpowder for flash, glass and metal plates; the whole works. But my real love? Music.

I played rock and roll in the 60's, and was somewhat of a local celebrity. I was actually offered a recording contract, but in the early 70's, my interest changed to classical music. I liked playing rock and roll music, because it made people want to move their bodies. But, I liked classical music even more, because

MACKINAC BRIDGE

Customer Fare Receipt

Lane 65    Collector 14

Class         Description
01   Car or Light Duty Truck

TOTAL FARE = $ 1.50

Date 09-05-2001   Time 12:12 PM

Buckle Up!

ked pure
sers like
write such
wanted to

lay toward
out of the
ple melody
ction came
ividly as if I
hearing a
r to me, and
re. It was like
fore, and yet
your life.

I didn't know wiry thin, the boat moved toward the island, I felt as if I were going home. And I felt like the symphony of my life, and the meaning of its notes, were becoming clear to me — finally.

*   *   *

As we reached the shores of Mackinac, I walked toward the front of the boat. I saw a small lighthouse on the starboard side. It must have been beautiful many years before, but now was neglected, and had fallen into serious disrepair. One corner of the lighthouse had completely caved in, and it looked as though the rest of the lighthouse would fall shortly.

"It's being restored," one of the deck-hands said, noticing that I was studying the lighthouse. "But they're still trying to figure out who's going to pay for it."

"How long has it been there?" I asked.

"I think it was built in the late 1800's. About the same time the houses up there on the west bluff were built," he said, pointing to the port side of the boat.

I looked to the north, and saw beautiful mansions lining the top of the hill, all the way down the hill to the majestic Grand Hotel.

"See the widows' walks?" he asked, pointing to the tops of the mansions.

"What?" I had no idea what he was talking about.

"The widows' walks. The towers and balconies on the cottages."

"You mean the mansions?" I asked.

"We call them cottages around here."

"Oh. So why are they called widows' walks?"

"It's kind of a carry over from the seaside houses. The wives of the sea captains would stand on the towers, and look out over the ocean, waiting for their husbands to return from sea."

"Were there any sea captains that lived in those houses?" I asked.

"I don't think so," he smiled, "but I think a few Great Lakes captains did. One for sure that I know of. Right there in the wedding cake house."

He pointed to one of the houses, and I could see immediately why he called it the wedding cake house. Its stories looked like the layers of a wedding cake, and the trim resembled lace-like decorations.

"He's kind of famous too, because he was murdered."

"Murdered? Wow! Murder on Mackinac. That would make a good book title," I said joking, thinking of what a nice ring it had to it.

"Yeah, it would. I've always wanted to be a writer. Maybe I'll write a book about it someday," he said, chuckling.

"And when was the Grand Hotel built?" I asked, looking at the beautiful building that was now directly on the port side.

"1886? 87? One of those years. They built it in three months," he said matter-of-factly.

"Wow!" I said. "So how many people live here?"

"Oh, only about four or five hundred year-rounders. But quite a few people just live here in the summer. Plus, the summer workers are starting to come in, and in a few weeks, hundreds of fudgies will be visiting the island."

"Fudgies?"

"Tourists. Visitors."

By this time we were pulling into the harbor.

"What should I do with my bags?"

"Where are you staying?"

"At the Murphy Hotel."

"You don't have to touch them. They'll be delivered right to your room. But it usually takes a little while to get them down there, so you might want to kick around downtown for a while."

"Thanks. So don't forget to write that murder mystery," I said, smiling at him as I stepped onto the dock.

"I just might do that," he laughed. "Oh, and the Murphy is just up to the street, and then take a right. You'll see it, just on the other side."

\* \* \*

When I reached the street, I was shocked to see no cars, only horses and carriages. It was too early to eat, and I didn't want to get to my hotel room before my bags got there. But I really didn't feel like exploring the downtown area. So I thought I'd walk by my hotel to see where it was, and then do a little exploring before supper.

I crossed the street and walked past the Murphy, just to establish home base, and then walked on toward the end of the block. When I got to the corner, I was totally in awe. On my right was an incredible view — a marina, the water, and the breakwaters. On my left, high on a hill, gleaming in the sun, were the white walls of a fort, complete with at least one cannon that I could see. At the base of the hill was a lush green park, filled with unblossomed lilac bushes. And in the center of the park was a large, dark statue.

I felt overwhelmed, because I realized that this was not a place I could explore in one hour, or even in one day. But it didn't matter. I had all the time in the world. I was unemployed. I had money in the bank. I could stay as long as I wanted. I no longer cared if I ever saw the island that my father had left to me. All I could think about was discovering this place.

I crossed the street and stood on the corner. I looked down the street that ran in front of the park, and there were several carriages, each with a sign that read: *For Hire.*

That's what I'll do, I thought. Spend what's left of the afternoon getting an overview of the island. Getting an idea of what I want to do for the next day, week, month.

As I crossed the street, I spotted a carriage driver who seemed to be an "old timer," and decided that he would probably know more about the island than any of the other drivers. I approached the driver, but before I had a chance to speak, he spoke.

"Where ya headed?" he asked me.

"Any place you want to show me," I answered. "I want to see the whole island."

"Well, we'll get a good start on. How's that?" he chuckled. "Hop aboard."

I stepped up onto the buggy, and sat back in the seat. The driver made a chick-chick sound with his teeth, and the team began to clip-clop down the street.

"So where ya from, young fella?" he asked, looking back over his shoulder.

"I was born and raised in Kansas. Lived in Ohio for a short while. How about you?"

"I was born in Missouri. Moved to Detroit when I was around twenty, and then moved up here about 30 years ago, in 1945. Still have some kin down state, but most have moved up north to get away from the crime."

"Yeah, it's getting bad all over. This seems like such a peaceful place. Bet you don't have much crime here."

"There's never any crime here. Oh, maybe a bike theft or two. Someone comes out of the bar too damned drunk to find their own bike, so they just grab the closest one they see."

"I heard you had a murder here once."

"We had *two* murders here. One about ten years ago. They never did solve that one. And the other one was seventy years ago. Nineteen-o-five. And they knew who did it, but they never did catch the fella . . . Watch the horses, please!" he yelled to a group of people walking down the middle of the street. "People think cuz there's no cars here they can just walk down the middle of the street," he said looking back over his shoulder at me.

"Fudgies. Isn't that what you call us?" I asked.

"I call 'em oblivions, from the planet oblivia. I don't know why we even bothered to make sidewalks. They don't use 'em anyway. You seem like a pretty smart fella, though. Just don't walk down the middle of the street, and you'll be ok," he said with a grin.

"So, anything else exciting happen here?" I asked.

"Well, we had a Hollywood movie made here in 46? 47? That guy with the big nose. You know: 'I got a million of em.' That guy. And the swimsuit girl."

"Yeah, I saw that movie when I was a kid."

"Some of the folks around here were extras in that movie," he paused. "And *most* of them didn't let it go to their heads," he said with a wink. "Most of the people around here are pretty levelheaded. Nice folks."

"So what's it like living here in the winter?" I asked him.

"I live in St. Ignace. You couldn't pay me enough to live here year round. I spent three winters here, and just about went stark raving mad."

"What about the summer, that must be nice?"

"Na! Too damned noisy."

"Must have been quiet at one time?"

"Oh, it used to be. But that was a long time ago. The same thing is happening everywhere. So-called modern progress seems to be giving us more ways to annoy our neighbors. And people can be annoying enough without needin' any tools to do it with. People just don't have any respect for each other nowadays."

"You can say that again. Wish we could go back to simpler times."

"We didn't appreciate those times when we had 'em, why would we appreciate 'em now?" he chuckled.

The whole time we'd been talking, I'd been looking at the beauty of this place, thinking about the innocence of times past, and wishing that I *could* go back to those times.

It took us about an hour and a half to travel the circumference of the island. When we arrived back at the park, it was close to five o'clock, and I was starving.

"Where's a good place to get something to eat?" I asked as I stepped down from the carriage.

"The Murphy. Best food on the island."

"Oh, good. That's where I'm staying."

"How long are you stayin' on the island, son?"

"I don't know. How long before the lilacs bloom?"

"I'd say about three weeks. Give or take a week."

"Guess I'm staying about three weeks. Give or take a week," I answered, smiling.

TWO

# Images from the Past

Walking into the Murphy was like stepping back in time. The sign on the outside said: *Established, 1883*. Inside, the carpets and drapes were dark, and the antique furniture was all turn of the century.

I would have checked in immediately, but as I walked to the front desk, I could see a sign at the end of a long hallway that read: *Restaurant*. I was famished, and there was no way I could even *consider* checking in until I had something to eat.

I started walking down the long hallway toward the restaurant, but as I did, I was overcome by the strangest feelings. I heard sounds: the clanking of dishes right beside me, but I could see no dishes; the sound of voices, but I saw no people. I felt like I was in a fun house at an amusement park; the farther I walked down the hallway, the longer the hallway seemed to become. And the worst part of it all was, that I felt like I was going through a gantlet; that there were people on both sides of the hall watching me. I was almost afraid to look at the walls for fear of what

I would see. And when I did, I felt chills run up my spine.

The walls were lined with pictures. Pictures of people. People long dead. Dead for many years. Pictures all taken on this island. Some probably taken in this very building.

I walked into the restaurant, and the feelings went as quickly as they came. I was greeted by a lovely young woman, tall and thin, with long blond hair.

"Hello. My name is Katia. Please follow me."

Her accent was a charming blend of Russian and Spanish, and as I followed her to my booth, I couldn't help but admire the gentle sway of her walk.

As I walked by each booth, I noticed pictures (like the ones I had seen in the hallway) hanging on the walls in each booth. Katia seated me in the fourth booth down, and handed me a menu.

"Your waitress will be right with you," she said, smiling sweetly.

She was beautiful. And normally, a smile like that would have summoned my noblest pursuit. But instead, I simply thanked her, and then enjoyed the view of her lovely figure as she walked away from my table, patting myself on the back for not trying to put the moves on her. My head just wasn't in that place, and I was so glad that it wasn't. The last thing on earth I needed was to get involved in a relationship. The very last thing.

I picked up the menu and was amazed at the variety of food. Everything: gourmet, home style, sandwiches, salads, drinks. Everything you could imagine. I was starving. And the roast beef sandwich with mashed potatoes and gravy looked great, but then, so did the planked whitefish. I could have roast beef anytime. I decided to celebrate my arrival on the Great Lakes with whitefish.

I looked to my right, only for a second, just to check out what condiments were on the table. Because no matter where I ate, or what I ordered, I had to have catsup. And as I looked that way, the picture on the wall caught my eye. It was like the other pictures I had seen on the walls. An old picture of people that lived long ago, dressed in turn of the century clothing. Nothing different, except . . .

I'd seen lots of old pictures before. Pictures from the 1890's, 1900's, 1910's, 20's. The men always looked so stern, and the women always looked, well . . . (there's no delicate way to put it) god-awful ugly.

When I was a child, my mother showed me pictures of my great-grandmother, and told me how beautiful she was. But I thought she looked like the bride of Frankenstein, or at least she looked like my great-grandfather.

I couldn't explain it. I knew hair styles had changed, and dress styles; all that. But *apart* from all that, it just seemed like women had gotten better looking through the years. Because I had never seen a beautiful woman in an old picture . . . until . . .

The picture was no different from any of the other old pictures I'd seen. This picture was taken on Mackinac Island, on the west bluff. I recognized the wedding cake house and the west end of the Grand Hotel in the background. It had one tall, stern man, and six women, plain women — ugly women — in the picture.

But on the far left side of the picture, was a young woman. A beautiful young woman. An incredibly beautiful young woman. And the strange thing was, she looked so familiar. So incredibly familiar. Like someone that I had known all my life. But I couldn't place her.

The photo was a reproduction of an old metal plate photo. It had a sepia toned finish, and yet, *she* seemed to be in color. I know it was only in my mind, but she seemed to light up the whole photo, and just for a moment, I could see her green checkered dress — *I know it was green* — waving in the wind.

Her hair was dark and full, and cascaded to her waist. Her skin was fair. Her face was slightly round, but mostly oval, and it seemed to glow with kindness. Her eyes were dark and big, and her eyelashes were long and dark. Her eyebrows were also dark, but not thick, and perfectly followed the line of her brow. Her cheeks seemed rosy, and her lips were full, and she was — so help me God — she was smiling!

"Can I start you out with a drink?"

"AH!" I blurted out, startled out of my trance by the waitress's question. As I tried to catch my breath, I looked around and noticed that everyone in the restaurant was looking at me. "Oh, God. I'm so sorry, but you scared the cra . . . you scared me."

"Can I get you something to drink?" she repeated quietly, intimidated by the scene I'd made.

"I'll just go ahead and order. I'll have the planked whitefish, fries, and a glass of wine. Merlot."

"What kind of dressing would you . . . ?"

"No salad, please. And could I have some tartar sauce on the side? I like it on the fries."

Like she needed to know, or cared, what I intended to do with the tartar sauce. Maybe I was afraid that she thought I'd be stupid enough to put tartar sauce on whitefish. Of course, maybe she thought it was more stupid to put it on my fries. Oh, God, what difference did it make what she thought.

"Oh, and some catsup too, please," I finished.

I looked back at the photo, and everything was back to the sepia tone. No color. But *she* was still beautiful. Still smiling.

As I sat there, I wondered how a photo like that ever came into existence. Did someone put an ad in the paper, saying: *Wanted: One stern looking man, six ugly women, and the most beautiful girl in the universe, to report to the west bluff for a photo*?

"Is everything all right? Do you need anything?"

I looked up to see Katia's lovely face. Apparently my outburst had upset the waitress more than I'd realized.

"Yes, there is. Could you possibly arrange for me to meet the photographer responsible for this photo? I'd like to sock him in the nose."

She laughed.

"Well, at least I'd like to sock him in the nose for seven-eights of the photo, anyway," I added, hoping to get some additional mileage from my quip.

She laughed again, and I felt at ease.

"I'm really sorry that I upset the waitress. I was just entranced by this photo, and I guess she startled me."

"She is lovely, isn't she? And I think a *lot* of people would have liked to have socked that photographer in the nose, but not because of his photography. He murdered a Great Lakes captain back in 1905."

"Oh, so *he's* the culprit. I heard they never caught the guy."

"Oh, yes they did. I thought they did. Maybe they did," she said, losing more confidence with each sentence. "Oh well. I'll have to brush up on my island history. I have to leave now, so if there is anything else you need, just let your waitress know."

"Out for a night on the town?" I quizzed.

"No, I have to work the front desk for a couple of hours," she said, sighing.

"Oh, good. I haven't checked in yet, so you'll get to see me again, I mean, I'll get to see *you* again."

"Well, Mr. . . . ?" she paused, waiting for my name.

"Bond, James Bond," I said, trying to keep a straight face. "Ok, Andrews, David Andrews," I said, finally giving up my true identity.

"Well, enjoy your dinner, David," she said with a smile. You know — *that* smile. Like I had a chance.

I did enjoy my dinner, being delighted by the charming company of the most beautiful woman in the world, one stern man, and six somewhat unattractive others. I paid my bill, left a rather large tip as a sin offering, and then proceeded to scoot to the end of the booth to stand up.

I was about halfway up when I saw a flash of light, and for just a moment, time seemed to be in *slow motion*. I heard the same sounds that I'd heard while walking down the hallway about an hour before. I looked down at the carpet. It changed color. It was different somehow. I looked up and saw someone sitting across from me at the table. It was a woman. In a dress. A turn of the century dress. And she had on a necklace. It was just a flash. Just a moment. And then it was gone.

I staggered as I stood. Everyone was looking at me again. One man whispered to his wife. I knew they thought I'd had too much to drink.

I walked up the hallway toward the front desk, and again I saw a flash. A young boy beside me, dressed in what I call a *monkey suit* (the old bellhop uniforms), dropped a stack of dishes. A man was yelling at him. People were laughing. And then, it was gone.

"I need some rest," I said to Katia as I approached the front desk.

"Just a second, I'll get your keys."

"Oh, and my bags."

"They're already in your room."

Katia walked ahead of me up the flight of stairs, and to the end of a hallway, to room 218. This all seemed so familiar to me somehow — no, not watching Katia's lovely walk from this perspective, though it was delightful, and becoming quite familiar

— but walking down this hallway. Walking to this room. So familiar.

"This is my favorite room," she said.

We walked into the room, and it began to happen again. Flashes. The wallpaper changed. The curtains changed. The carpet changed. The furniture changed. And then back again.

"Oh, wow! I *do* need some rest," I said, sitting down on the bed, before I *fell* down.

Katia walked to the door, and then looked back at me.

"I'm not supposed to do this, I mean, go out with the guests. But, I get off at eight. Maybe we could grab a drink or something," she said with *that* smile.

Under other circumstances, I would have jumped at the chance to take this lovely girl out. But I was dead tired, and worn out from the events of the day. Besides, I was in love. With the woman in the picture.

"Thanks for the offer, but I'm dead. Maybe a rain check?"

"Sure. How long are you staying?"

"Till the lilacs bloom," I said without missing a beat.

"Good," she said, smiling. Then she turned, and with a deliberate flip of her hair, was out of the room.

\* \* \*

As weird as the evening had been, I thought I would have had dreams, nightmares, and a lousy night's sleep. But, I slept like a log. The only time I woke up, was to the sound of a freighter's horn as it made its way through the Straits of Mackinac. And *that* didn't even bother me. It was more comforting than anything. Oh, and I did wake once to some drunk on the street singing the *Star-Spangled Banner*. But I just laughed myself back to sleep.

The morning light began to peek in my window, and I thought about getting out of bed. But the sound of the water beating against the shore was so soothing. Then I heard the clip-clop of the horses in the street, and wished that I had woken up in 1905. I would go see *her*. The most beautiful — and probably the most charming — woman in the entire world.

\*   \*   \*

When I'd arrived on the ferry the day before, I'd seen boys jumping off the docks into the icy Lake Huron waters, and I promised myself that I would do that, at least once, while visiting here. That morning, I decided, would be the morning. I put on my cutoffs, a T-shirt, and some old tenny runners, and headed for the docks.

I knew if I thought about it too long, that I'd talk myself out of it. So I just did it. Just jumped, before I had a chance to think. It was exhilarating.

\*   \*   \*

Breakfast that morning was uneventful. No flashes. No sounds. And the hostess had seated me in a different booth than the night before, so, no *woman of my dreams*, either. The booth I sat in had an old photo also, but it didn't matter. I wasn't interested in it. *She* wasn't in it.

After breakfast, I decided that I would explore the island some more. I had been *around* the island. Now I would explore the *interior* of the island. As I walked out the door, I met Katia coming into work.

"Out so early?" she asked.

"Yeah, I want to get an early start exploring the island."

"Make sure you make it up to Arch Rock. Oh, and Skull Cave too."

"I was thinking about taking a tour. Is it worth it?" I asked her.

"They're ok, but definitely do some exploring on your own. Speaking of exploring, I have the night off, and it's Friday, and I was wondering if you'd like to use your rain check?"

There was that smile again. And before I even had a chance to think about what I was saying, I answered.

"Yeah, sure. Eight o'clock?"

"Eight's a date," she said, smiling, and doing the flip thing with her hair again.

Maybe I should have said no. Told her, *Sorry, but I'm in love with another woman. She lives in 1905, nevertheless . . .*

Oh, yeah. That would have gone over real well. Anyway, Katia was sweet. Pretty and confident. I liked that. Besides, what was I going to do for the next two or three weeks while I waited for the lilacs to bloom? Be an antisocial pain for the whole wait? It wasn't like we were going to get married or anything. And it's not like I had much of a chance with Miss 1905. It was just a date. A drink.

\*   \*   \*

The tour was only supposed to be a couple of hours long, but the group was mostly seniors, which slowed things down considerably.

First, the carriages took us to the highest point on the island: Fort Holmes. As I stood atop the fort and looked out across the waters at the Mackinac Bridge, I was amazed at its beauty and grandeur. What a feat it must have been to build it, or to even conceive that it *could* be built. And how different life must have been before it was built. I couldn't imagine what it was like to look out over the water and not see it there. It just seemed to fit there.

At Arch Rock, our tour guide showed us a photo of President Ford as a Boy Scout, standing out on the arch. I thought of how he had fallen down an airplane ramp on national television just a few weeks before.

"Boy, someone was watching over that klutz," one of the seniors commented.

When we got to Skull Cave, our guide talked about how in the 1800's, a soldier had hidden in the cave to escape capture, and when he awoke the next morning, he was surrounded by skulls. I thought of how strange that must have been. Right out of a *Twilight Zone* episode. Something about this place intrigued me, and I decided to stay behind, and start exploring on my own.

There was a large sign in front of the cave that read: *STAY OUT;* and on the sides, a sign that read: *STAY OFF THE ROCKS.*

I waited until the group was out of sight, and then quickly went inside the cave. It was nothing spectacular, so I decided to climb around on the rocks above. I climbed to the top of the rocks, and sat under the trees that grew out of the top. It was so quiet and peaceful, I could have stayed there all day. But then I did something really stupid. I was sweating from the climb to the top of the rocks, and my leather watch band began to irritate my wrist. So I took off my watch. When I went to put it back on, I dropped it over the side of the rocks.

I looked over the side, and about five feet down, was a small opening in the rocks. And, to my misfortune, the watch had fallen inside the opening. I climbed down the rocks, and looked inside the opening, but I couldn't see the watch.

I would have left it, but it was my father's watch. Not a postinheritance watch, either. But a watch that he had left behind when he went to the ball game that day, when I was four. I don't know why it meant so much to me. I mean, it shouldn't have, after what he'd done. But quite honestly, that watch meant more to me than anything I'd inherited from my father. I had to get that watch.

The opening was barely large enough for a child to squeeze into, so there was no way *I'd* be able to. I put my arm and shoulder into the opening, and began to feel around. Just then I felt something move.

"SCREECH!" came a sound out of the opening.

"WHAT IN THE . . . ?" I pulled my hand quickly out of the hole. And as soon as I had, a squirrel came running out of the hole, and up the rocks, into the trees.

"You little bastard! You scared the crap out of me!" I yelled up the tree.

Once I had convinced myself that I wouldn't be confronted by any other varmint, I reached my arm and shoulder in again, and began to feel around. Finally, I felt what I was sure was my watchband. But just the tip of it. I couldn't quite reach it. I knew if I could just stretch my arm another quarter of an inch, I'd have it.

I stretched my arm practically out of socket, and I put my shoulder against the rocks, and put all my weight against the opening. Then suddenly, it happened. The rocks gave way, and I went tumbling into the opening, head first.

Bam! I hit my head on a rock.

"Dag Nab it!" I shouted. Those weren't the first words that came to my mind, nor were they the first out of my mouth. But my mother had always said that cursing was a failure of the imagination. And I felt that she would have been proud of me, considering the situation, for at least having the presence of mind to get it right the second time.

There was my watch right in front of me. But in front of the watch was something that literally made me forget the watch entirely.

### THREE

# A Crack in Time

There, engraved in the stone wall before me, were these words and symbols:

TEMPORALIS FISSVRA

LXX

~>~

When I was twelve, I had a friend whose dad chiseled names and dates in gravestones. He was eventually put out of work by technology. But we would watch him work for hours. The engraving in the stone was definitely the work of someone who knew what they were doing. Very clean.

I was pretty rusty on my Latin, but I knew the first word had to do with time: *that belonging to the temporal.* But the second word I didn't recognize. Underneath were engraved the Roman numerals, LXX. Underneath that was the mathematical symbol for *greater than.* This all fascinated me. But what fascinated me the most was what was on both sides of the *greater than* symbol. It was the symbol for *infinity.*

I had always been fascinated by numbers and mathematics. Mathematical links, both intricate and simple, abound in the physical universe.

Most of my time in college was spent studying subjects not on the curriculum. While I sat in classes and lectures, I would study what was of interest to me, while pretending to take notes. My love for music extended into a fascination with the *physics* of music. I wanted to understand the science behind it. I wanted to know *why* notes harmonized, not just *that* they harmonized. And this led to my fascination with numbers, and number patterns, in the physical universe.

For example, there are seven primary tones in the diatonic major scale. There are also seven major colors in the light spectrum. And the mathematical relationships of the notes that harmonize, and the colors that harmonize, are the same. The plant kingdom has certain numbers that tend to dominate, as does the animal kingdom, and the insect kingdom.

I studied other — seemingly unconnected — categories, to observe number patterns. And I found more and more connections, from the simple to the complex. The more connections I found, the more intrigued I became.

A numeric harmony seemed to permeate the natural universe, making the whole universe harmonize in a sequence of mathematical relationships. I had often theorized that the basis for matter itself, was a sequence of vibration and number patterns, and that numbers *themselves* have intrinsic worth and meaning.

I sat there in amazement, looking at the writing on the stone, wondering what it all meant. I had no idea. But I wasn't supposed to be there. The signs said so. And I was going to leave. But just as I turned to leave, I heard those sounds again, like the ones I heard in the hallway of the hotel. I turned back toward the stone, and I could see a faint beam of light, pouring through one edge of the stone.

I could now see that there was dried clay around the edges of the stone, sealing it to the wall. I picked up a sharp rock and began to dig at the clay around the edges, and as I did, more light began to pour in. The more I dug, the more the covering began to move. My heart was pounding as I removed the last bit of clay holding the stone in place. I wondered what I would find. A grave? Maybe a treasure? I pulled the stone from the wall.

"Oh, great. A hole," I said aloud.

I'd found a hole. It was just a hole to the back side of the rocks. That was the "white light." I could see all the way through to the back of the rocks. Woop-dee-do. A hole.

"Oh, well. No big deal," I thought. I'd just climb down through the hole and out the backside of the rocks. But when I climbed down through the hole, the strangest feeling went through my body; like life had just jumped down two octaves. That's the only way I know how to describe it. It was like every atom in the universe had just reduced its vibrational speed by half, and then by half again.

The colors around me became blurred. And the sounds around me resembled a recording being played at half speed, and then down at half *that* speed. It felt like I had traveled back to my old hippy days, and was on an acid trip.

In a few moments, the world around me came back up to speed; quickly, but incrementally noticeable, like someone turning the pitch control on a reel to reel tape machine back up to speed in steps. Yet, it seemed like it was just a hair shy of being up to speed.

I was drained. Just like I'd been the day before, when I'd heard the sounds and seen the flashes in the restaurant. I just wanted to go back to my room and rest. I dusted myself off and started to walk around the front of the rocks to the road. But the sound of a horse whinny stopped me in my tracks. I knew I'd been caught.

I was sure that when I looked up I would see a park ranger, or police officer, and would have to pay a fine, or worse. But instead what I saw was a carriage full of . . . well, really strange people. The thing that was so strange about them was, that they were all wearing turn of the century costumes.

I would have loved to have traveled back in time to simpler times. And I'd thought about that very thing more than once since I had arrived on Mackinac Island. But this was ridiculous. These people were living in a fantasy. All I could think was, "People, get a life." And the really funny thing about it was, these people would have fit right in with the turn of the century, because, the man in the carriage looked so stern, and the women with him were homely as hell. But what made the whole experience even more strange was, the way they were looking at me. Like *I* was weird. Like there was something wrong with *me*.

Granted, I was rather disheveled, dirty, and sweaty from climbing around on the rocks. But this was just plain weird. I just wanted to go back to the room, and get some rest. And then I remembered. My watch! It was still up inside the opening.

As soon as they had passed by, I climbed up the back of the rocks. And as I passed through the opening in the rocks, I felt a tingling sensation pass through my body. Everything speeded up this time, instead of slowing down. And as before, I became accustomed to the atmosphere, except this time everything came *completely* back up to speed.

"What a strange experience," I thought.

I carefully picked up the stone with the engraving on it, and placed it back over the opening of the hole. I hoped that no one would notice I had moved it. But who was I kidding. No one could have gotten in there to begin with, so how would anyone know I'd messed with it.

\*     \*     \*

I made it back to my hotel room around five, and was totally exhausted. I would have gone right to bed, but taking a shower gave me a second wind. I decided that I would go downstairs and have something to eat before retiring.

I went downstairs, and down the long hallway to the restaurant. No sounds or strange feelings this time. I wanted to sit in *my* booth, so I could gaze at her picture. But unfortunately, someone was already seated there.

After I ordered, I became very tired again, and would have gone up to my room. But I looked up to the old photo on the wall in my booth. And suddenly my whole afternoon took on a new dimension, and I completely forgot about how tired I was.

There on the wall was an old picture of a horse and carriage. The people in the carriage were wearing turn of the century clothing. The man was stern looking, and the women were homely. Pretty much like the other photos. But, these people were familiar. And they didn't just *seem* familiar. They *were* familiar. These were the *same* people that I had encountered that afternoon at Skull Cave.

Feelings of shock went over my body, then disbelief, then fear. I was afraid. Either I was going crazy, or . . .

I knew what was happening. I knew what this meant. I thought about the words on the stone, TEMPORALIS FISSURA, and suddenly, I understood their meaning. FISSURA! Fissure. A fissure! A fissure — a crack — in time! Someone — at least one — before me, had found it, and had gone through it. Someone had engraved those words on that stone, and covered the opening with it. But why did they cover it? And were the words a directive, or a warning? And what was the meaning of the other symbols engraved on the stone?

I left the restaurant immediately, forgetting all about the food I'd ordered. I walked out of the hotel and into the street, and instead of heading toward the park, I headed the opposite direction, toward the west end of the island. I just wanted to think. To think about *why* I had done all that I had done that day. *What* had led me to that stone? So many things had happened in my life to bring me to this island. My whole life seemed to be a journey to this destination.

I walked along the beach until sunset. It was the most beautiful sunset I had ever seen. Overhead, the sky was blue, to dark blue. And toward the bridge, near the horizon, the sky was bright orange, graduating to red, then purple, and then blue, the higher it went. And it was constantly changing, so that, each time I thought I couldn't stand any more of its glory, it became even more glorious.

As it got dark, I looked across the water at the lighthouse; dead, dark, and decaying. I looked at the lights on the bridge; modern, but bright and beautiful. The contrast saddened me.

It was so peculiar that, as soon as I had realized the meaning of the words on the stone, that I had gone to the opposite end of the island from the stone. Almost as if I was trying to get away from the place, from the truth, from the inevitable. It was waiting there for me, and I *knew* it was waiting there. For me. Just me. Others may had found it in *their* time, but I had found it in mine. It was waiting for me, and I knew that I had to go back through it — that very night.

\* \* \*

I could hardly see as I made my way up the hill toward Skull Cave. I had never been so anxious about anything in all my life. On my way, I saw someone coming down the hill with a flashlight, and I moved into the woods and hid behind a large tree until they passed.

I had to go back through the time fissure, if only for a few hours. I would go to town, in the shadow of the night, and see what the past looked like. What it felt like.

I climbed up the rocks, feeling my way in the darkness, almost falling twice, because I couldn't see to get a handhold. I thought about what I would do if I were to be spotted in the past. What if a policeman, or a constable, or whatever they had back then, saw me, or questioned me? What would I do if I had to make a quick getaway? What if the roads and trails that I had walked that day weren't there in the past? And where in the past was I going? To what year? Day? Month?

By the time I climbed up the rocks, I had just about talked myself out of going through the time portal. And then I remembered — *the picture! Her* picture. *She* might be there!

With that thought, every fear disappeared. I removed the engraved stone from the opening, took a breath, and went through. I felt the same feelings I had felt earlier; like the whole universe had dropped down an octave, and then an octave again. Except this time the world around me came back up to speed more quickly (or I had simply become acclimatized to it faster).

It was pitch dark as I stumbled around to the front side of the rocks. And I probably wouldn't have been able to even find my way to town, only, about every seven or eight seconds, I saw a faint light in the distant sky. Though I couldn't see its source, I knew where the light was coming from. It was the lighthouse. She was alive, and in her youth. She was guiding sailors through the Straits of Mackinac, and on this night, she was helping a time traveler find his way in the dark.

I knew from the people that I had seen that day, the people in the photograph, that I was somewhere around the turn of the century. I'd read that the fort was closed and turned over to the State Park Commission in 1895. But I wasn't sure what year I was in, so I walked as quietly as I could until I passed the fort.

Once I got past the fort, I rested next to an old wooden fence. The fence surrounded the area where the park was supposed to be. Except, there wasn't a park there, and no ominous statue either. Just a large field that looked like it was perhaps a large vegetable garden. And I could see by the dim lights of the downtown area that there was no marina either, and no breakwater. Just open water.

I walked to the street, and felt a gravel-like substance under my feet. It wasn't asphalt, but it didn't feel like dirt either. Maybe it *was* dirt, just packed hard from traffic.

I crossed the street and stood by the beach where the marina was in my time, and every seven or eight seconds the light from the lighthouse would light up the waterfront. I could see the dock where I got off the ferry, and the coal dock down just a little farther. As far as I could tell in the dim light, they looked virtually the same.

As I walked back to the street to head toward town, something was blowing down the street; blowing directly toward me, as though some unseen hand were guiding it. I reached down and picked it up. It was the front page of a newspaper, *The Advertiser's Gazette*, and the date on the front was, *May 16, 1905.*

If this paper was current, then everything made sense. It seemed new. Why wouldn't it be a current paper? Maybe even that day's. Its date was the same as the day I'd just been in, in 1975. This was exactly seventy years earlier — *to the day!* LXX. Seventy. Seventy years! That was it. I had traveled seventy years into the past, to the very day! Probably to the very minute!

I folded the newspaper, put it into my jacket pocket, and headed down the street toward town. I looked at the first building on the water side of the street. A sign on the side of the building read: *The Chippewa Cafe*. The building looked like it had just been built within the last two or three years. I walked past the front of the building, and there was a sign that read: *The Chippewa Hotel*.

As I walked down the streets of Mackinac Island, I felt invincible. I made no attempt to hide myself. There was no word to describe how I felt. Exhilarated comes close. But maybe the best word is — dare I use this word —*fun!* It was fun. Fun being in the past. Fun knowing so many things that were going to happen in the future. Fun walking around knowing all this stuff that no one else on this Island knew. Fun.

I walked down the street toward the west end of the island, and didn't see a single soul. It was so quiet that, at one point, I thought I must be dreaming, else, I would have seen someone. And at just that moment, I heard the familiar clip clop behind me; a dray turning the corner at Astor Street onto Main, heading away from me, back toward the park.

When I got to the beach on the southwest end of the island, it was like someone had knocked the wind right out of me. I looked off across the water, and there was no bridge. Only a few hours before, I had thought about how the decaying lighthouse contrasted with the newness of the bridge. Now I stood there with the newness of the newborn light house, in contrast to . . . to *no* bridge. It felt so strange.

More than anything, I wanted to stay there until the sun rose, to see a 1905 sunrise. I walked the length of the shore, to Mission Point, and stayed until almost 5:45 a.m., It was the most glorious sunrise I had ever seen. Maybe it was just my state of mind, but it seemed so different than a 1975 sunrise. More pure. More clean. I don't know what it was. It was just magnificent.

Suddenly I realized that people would be getting up all over town. They would see me. In my 1975 clothes. That was not good. Not good at all.

I headed back to town, and just as I got to the park, I was met by a boy selling newspapers. He looked at me like he'd just seen a ghost, or something queerer. I shot up the hill as quick as I could.

As I ran up the hill, I thought of the newspaper page that was in my jacket pocket, and wondered why I was even going back to 1975. I could work for the newspaper. I had the skills. I could come back to 1905 and live.

It was a compelling thought, but I knew I had to get back to my own time. If I really wanted to live in the past, I needed to do some preparation, and plenty of it. I needed clothes and money that predated 1905. I needed to read up on my island history. I needed . . . oh, hell, I needed some sleep.

FOUR

# Preparing for the Past

When I arrived back in 1975, I stood outside the Murphy, and looked down the street that I'd walked down several hours before, or should I say, seventy years before. Some things had changed, but basically it was still the same.

I'd seen pictures of my hometown in Kansas from around the turn of the century. But by the 50's, the town looked totally different. As a child, I frequented an old general store on the corner of my block. It had a worn planked floor, and a pickle barrel that sat by the front door. I'd get a pickle, or some candy, and then go across the street to the train station, to watch people get on and off the trains. Both the general store and the train station were gone by the 60's. Most places change. But not Mackinac Island. At least, it certainly didn't seem to change as quickly as the rest of the world.

But I had done enough reflecting. I had a big day ahead of me, preparing to return to 1905, and I needed some rest.

I walked through the front door of the Murphy, and there at the front desk, in tears, was Katia.

"Oh, my God. Katia."

I couldn't believe that I had forgotten all about our date. I could only imagine what she must have thought of me.

"Katia, I'm so sorr . . ."

"You jerk. If you don't want to go out with me, just say so."

"It's not like that. I . . ."

"Hope you had a good time, with whoever she was," she said crying, as she walked away from the front desk, and into the ladies room.

I knew I had really messed up, but there was no way I could deal with this now. I had just traveled seventy years into the past, and back again. I had discovered the secret. I had to go back again.

After getting a few hours of sleep, I went to the local library, and read everything I could find regarding the island's history. Particularly 1905. I knew the thing I would have to be the most careful about, was referring to events that hadn't happened yet, or things that didn't yet exist.

Also, my speech patterns. On the tour, the day before, I'd had a conversation with a lady who'd been an extra in *This Time for Keeps*. I commented on how stilted I felt the dialog was in the movie. But she assured me that, *that was the way people spoke back then*. I realized one of the major things that would make me stand out to the people in 1905, would most likely be my speech patterns.

My speech was fairly free of the idiomatic phrases of the late 60's, early 70's — far out, out of sight, groovy — as I had rejected the language, along with the whole so-called *rebellion against the establishment*; especially when the rebellion became its *own* "establishment." But what if the occasional unfiltered idiom cropped up? Like, if I referred to a Coca-Cola as a Coke. I wasn't even sure when Coke was invented. What if I referred to an automobile as a car? That wouldn't be too much of a problem, as I knew cars had been banned from the island before 1905. At least I thought so.

I needed much more time to study. And not just the island's history, but history in general, and the speech and idioms of the time, and the economics of the time, and the politics, and the . . . oh, a *million* other things. But in the back of my mind, I was afraid that I would go up the hill, and the time portal would be gone. I was so anxious about getting back to 1905, that I must admit, my research was cursory, at best.

And beyond simple anxiety, I felt the pressing need to go back, right away. Like I was *supposed* to be there, and soon. It was more like a nagging, that if I didn't get there soon, something awful was going to happen. I didn't have any more time left for history lessons. I knew I'd have to get them first hand.

The clothing was actually not that difficult to locate, nor was currency and coins from the day. I actually got a great deal on well-worn, unrare currency. And that is exactly what I needed. Money that looked like it had been used, and coins and currency that weren't particularly rare, so that I wouldn't have to pay a premium for them.

I ate lunch and dinner away from the hotel, and when I went back to my room, I went up through the back fire exit. It was an awful thing to do, but I just couldn't handle seeing Katia again.

As I sat at my desk that evening, I thought about whether or not I *should* go back to 1905. What if I traveled back, and couldn't get back to my own time? What if I didn't want to come back? What if I got there and *she* wasn't there? What if I did something that totally screwed up history? What if I could change history? Should I? The Titanic disaster would occur just seven years after I arrived. Should I try to stop it? What if a mass-murderer died on that boat, and I were to save him? What if a scientist was on that boat, that would help Hitler develop the rocket before the end of the war, and the Nazis ended up winning World War II?

My mind was reeling. I had to stop thinking about it. I knew that if I did go back to 1905, I would have to be very careful. But then, what if in being careful, I didn't do something that I *should* do. If I went back, would I alter my own existence?

"Shut up, brain!" I shouted aloud. "I'm going, and that's that."

*   *   *

It was about five o'clock Sunday morning when I went through the portal. It was May 18th, 1905.

I wanted to arrive on a Sunday morning, to go to one of the local churches; someplace where a good number of townspeople would be congregated, and get an idea of who was who. I had my choice of denominations, and since I was never really a church goer, I thought I'd pick the church that interested me the most. The Little Stone Church. It had just been built, and I wanted to see how much it had changed by 1975.

I waited until almost nine o'clock that morning, and then made my way down the back trail, behind the Grand Hotel, and down Grand Hill. When I arrived at the church, I thought that I had arrived late. There was no one outside, and I heard no singing inside. I assumed they were praying, and I hesitated to open the door, knowing it would probably creak. I certainly didn't want to bring any more attention to myself than I had to. Finally, I summoned the nerve to open the door. The large door creaked, and the sound echoed loudly through the sanctuary. I closed my eyes as I stepped in, knowing that every eye would be on me. But when I opened my eyes, there was no one there. Not a soul.

"What in the . . . ?" My words echoed off the walls.

I didn't understand. What had I done wrong? I had arrived on Mackinac Island on a Thursday, came back the first time to 1905 on Friday, prepared for my trip on Saturday. "It's Sunday," I thought. "It has to be."

I wondered if I had miscalculated. If somehow, the newspaper I'd found in the street wasn't current.

I had it in my coat pocket. I pulled it out immediately to inspect it. It read: *May 16th, 1905*. Only I had neglected to notice one very important detail: *Tuesday, May 16th, 1905*.

"Of course. The day of the week."

I had come back exactly seventy years. To the day. Probably even to the minute. But the day of the week was different. It was Thursday in 1905. Thursday, May 18th, 1905.

I was born on a Thursday, and ever since I was a child, I had liked Thursday. More than any other day of the week. And I didn't know why. I liked the way it sounded. The way the word looked on a page. I just liked Thursday. Just like I had a favorite spoon when I was a child. Just like the color blue-green. I couldn't explain why it had always been my favorite color. It just was. Same with Thursday.

Through no plan of my own, I had arrived on Mackinac Island on a Thursday. And now, quite *contrary* to my planning, I had arrived to live in 1905, also on a Thursday. Strange.

# Living in
# the Past

FIVE

# A New Beginning

I had arrived in 1905, and suddenly my fears about not being able to get back to 1975, or about doing something stupid that would change history, vanished. I felt like I was at home. Like I was *supposed* to be here. And besides, what did I have to go back to 1975 for, anyway? Nothing.

I walked down Grand Hill to Market Street, then to Hoban, and over to Main. As I walked down Main, I noticed a group of old timers sitting in front of one of the buildings, chatting and chewing tobacco. The sign on the front of the building said: *U.S. Post Office.* And I remembered reading that the post office had been on the main street many years before it was moved to Market Street. One of the old timers said, "Good morning," to me. And I smiled and said, "Good morning," right back.

As I walked down the street, I felt completely comfortable. People smiled and said "Good morning." No one looked at me like I was out of place, or as if I didn't belong. I guess they were so accustomed to tourists on the island, that one more didn't stand out.

I'm not sure why I hadn't noticed before, but suddenly I realized that electric poles and wires lined the streets. They looked so out of place. They weren't there in 1975. You'd think it would be the other way around. How strange.

I knew that if I were to stay in 1905, I would need to find someplace to live right away. The local newspaper was already my target for a job. But I was confident that, even if it fell through, I could get a job somewhere washing dishes — a job I was quite familiar with from my college days at Cornell University.

I was concerned that my cash would be used up quickly if I stayed in a hotel. But I knew I'd have a better chance of getting good permanent housing if I had a job first. So I decided that I would stay at the Murphy until I landed a job, then find something permanent; perhaps a cabin.

I walked up to the front of the Murphy, and looked up at the building. It looked virtually the same, except, the sign on the front read: *The New Murphy*. "Ha!" I laughed aloud. "How ironic," I thought, as I walked into the lobby and up to the front desk.

The lobby looked so similar to the 1975 version, that for a moment, I half-expected Katia to come to the front desk. But to my relief, a middle-aged gentleman stepped forward.

"May I help you, sir?" he asked.

"Yes, I need a room."

"Just for the night, or will you be staying longer?"

I picked up on his tone, that longer meant, *much* longer.

"Well, I'm working here this summer, and looking for something . . ."

"We have monthly rates available," he said, interrupting me, like he'd already dealt with a hundred people in just my situation.

He gave me the monthly rate, and I swear, I almost fell over. It was so minuscule. I suddenly felt very insecure about the money I had in my suitcase. I realized that, what I had felt was a good amount of money to bring with me, was in fact, an *exorbitant* amount of money. I had failed to take into consideration how much more this currency would buy in 1905.

I suddenly realized that I was (for all practical purposes) a rich man, and could have bought a house, had I wanted to. Of course, I didn't want to. I wanted to work, and blend in. I knew I would have to keep my relative affluence a secret. Luckily, I had a small amount of money in my wallet, and didn't have to open my suitcase to pay for the room.

"Did you fall in the water?" the desk clerk asked laughing, looking at the condition of the currency that I'd handed him.

At first I didn't understand his comment, but then I realized, my currency was more than seventy-five-years-old!

"Oh, yeah, I had a little accident," I said, trying to justify the currency's condition.

"Could you please sign here, Mr. . . . ?" He pushed the guest book toward me and waited for my reply.

I don't know why, but for some reason, I just felt that I shouldn't give my real name. But I didn't know what name to give. At that moment, a childhood incident flashed to my mind.

I was fifteen years old, and my friend Ken Steiger and I were out on Halloween night. We were decorating houses with toilet paper, had just decorated our eighth or ninth house of the evening, and were feeling pretty good about ourselves. We were on our last house of the evening, when, out of the house came a big burly guy; about three hundred pounds, and all muscle. We knew we were had.

He said he was going to report us to the police, and he wanted to know our names. Ken, like a real pro, said, "My name is," and then gave this guy some name I had never heard of before. Then the guy asked me my name. I just freaked. I knew I couldn't give him my real name, so I didn't. I looked at him and said, "My name is Ken Steiger." I had given him my friend's name. Duh!

"Your name, sir?" I was summoned back to reality by the sound of the desk clerk's voice.

"David . . ." Oh, God! I'd given him my real first name. I had to think fast. I looked out the front window, to a sign that was hanging across the street: *Candy Creme Soda. Try it. You'll love it!*

"Lovit. David Lovit," I said, and quickly signed the book.

"Your room is 218," he said, and then motioned to one of the bellhops seated across the room. "Thomas, please take Mr. Lovit to room 218."

As I walked up the stairs I felt . . . I felt a sense of déjá vu of déjá vu — if that makes any sense. Only a few days before, I had walked up these stairs with Katia, and had felt as if I'd done this before. Now, only a few days later; or should I say seventy years before? Or should I say . . . ? Oh, it was all too weird for me.

I walked into the room. Except for a large armoire on one side of the room, the furniture was different than in 1975. But it all looked familiar. And then I remembered why. I remembered the flashback I'd had when I first stepped into this room with Katia. The carpets, the drapes, the furniture. Everything. Just the way I'd seen it in my flashback; or whatever it was.

"If there is anything else, sir, please just let me know," Thomas said, his hand outstretched.

I knew he was waiting for a tip, and I almost handed him a five-dollar bill. But before I did, I realized my error, and tried to do some quick math in my head, comparing the room rates with 1975 rates, and then tipping an appropriate proportion.

I handed him two 1904 quarters.

"Thank you, sir!" he said, like I'd just handed him a couple of gold pieces.

I realized that the tip must have been too generous. But it was too late, and there was nothing I could do about it. He walked to the door, opened it, and then stopped. He looked down at the tarnished quarters, then up at me. "Sir, did you fall in the water?"

"Long story, kid. Very long story."

\* \* \*

After the bellhop left, I went right to bed. I slept all through the afternoon and night, and didn't wake up till about five o'clock Friday morning.

When I awoke, I heard the sound of a freighter's horn as it made its way through the Straits. I thought that it had all been a dream, but when I looked out the window across the street, I saw the Chippewa, newly built, and the dirt streets, and the old style buggies. It was real. It was 1905.

I'd been so tired the night before, that I'd gone to bed without using the facilities. And now, I had to go rather urgently. I soon realized, however, that what had been the door to my bathroom in 1975, was now the door to a closet. And I realized it just in time.

I ran out the door of my room, and my timing couldn't have been better. I saw a gentleman walking out of a door, just down the hallway. He easily sensed my dilemma, considering that I was bent over in pain.

"Right here, man," he said, and pointed to the door he had just exited.

"Bless you, sir," I said as I ran into the room.

I looked around the bathroom and saw a large porcelain bathtub with hot and cold running water. But no shower. I couldn't help but think about how much I hated taking baths as a child, and of the joy I experienced when I left for college, and I had my first shower. I swore I would never take another bath as long as I lived. I even dreaded visiting my mom, because she didn't have a shower.

Well, I didn't have a choice now. A bath it would have to be.

After bathing and getting dressed for the day, I headed down the stairs to the restaurant. It was somewhat different than in 1975. But yet, in many ways, it was still the same. The booths were there (but the wood was newer, of course), and they were covered with colorful fabric.

Though the manner of the people was quite different, they didn't seem to mind my differences in speech and custom. Mackinac was accustomed to people from all over the country and world.

At one point, while having breakfast that morning, I heard the couple next to me arguing over whether I was from North Carolina, or Ireland. At about that same time, the waitress showed up with my breakfast, and asked me where I was from.

I'd thought about what I'd say if asked that question, and knew if I said some big city, that sooner or later I'd run into someone who'd say, "Oh, I'm from there. What part? What street? What house? Do you know so and so?" So to avoid being caught in that trap, I had already rehearsed what I'd say.

"Oh, way out in southwest Kansas. On the plains. Way, way, way out on the plains," I answered the waitress.

"Oh, I've never been to Kansas," she answered. I was glad she had never been there. I was also glad that the couple next to me had overheard our conversation, and had stopped discussing where I was from.

*   *   *

After breakfast, the first order of business was to find a job. I hated job hunting. It was too much like sales; walking up to a total stranger, and trying to convince them that they needed what you had to sell. I'd been involved once in a get-rich-quick scheme, going door to door selling vacuum cleaners. After that experience, I swore I'd never get involved in sales again, as long as I lived. And to me, job searching was just a little too akin to sales for my comfort.

I walked through the front door of the Advertiser's Gazette. It was one large room. On my left was a waiting area, with chairs and a small table. And on my right was a rail banister, that divided the waiting area from the several desks that made up the office area.

In the back were several typesetting desks and a large printing press. The press was being run by a boy that couldn't have been more than seventeen. A large man, maybe ten years older than I, was inspecting copies (of what looked like posters) as they came off the press. He had red hair, and looked like he was of Scottish descent.

The man walked over to the divider, glanced up at me, and then looked back down at his poster.

"Can I help you?" he asked, over the loud clanking of the press, still looking down at the poster.

"I'm looking for a job."

"What?"

"I'm looking for a job."

"What? I can't hear you."

He walked over to one of the desks, picked up a newspaper, and folded it over several times. He then walked over to the boy, and *whapped* him on top of the head with it.

"Can't you see I'm trying to talk to this gentleman?" he yelled at the boy.

The boy turned off the press, as the man walked back to me.

"You're looking for a job. I don't need anybody," he said curtly, and started walking back to the press.

"I can write, typeset, run a press . . ."

"Ever done any reporting?" he said, cutting me off.

"That's my long-suit."

"I don't need anybody," he said, then walked over to the press and started it again.

"I'm a good photographer," I yelled over the sound of the press.

As soon as the words came out of my mouth, he shut off the press again.

"A photographer, hey?"

The boy had a huge smirk on his face, and blurted out, "He's blown himself up twice with the flash powder."

The man picked up the folded paper, and hit the boy over the head again. "Shut up you little bastard," he yelled at the boy. The boy went back behind the press, but still had the smirk on his face.

"Yes, sir. A photographer. And I do good work," I said.

He walked over and stood directly in front of me. "Are you good with the flash powder?" he asked, with one eye closed, and his head cocked sideways.

By this time I'd gleaned that his accent had subtle hints of Irish and Scottish.

"Rand Linn," he said, and stretched out his hand.

"David Lovit," I answered, shaking his hand.

"Well, Lovit, when can you start to work?"

"Right now."

"Good, good. I like a man who doesn't procrastinate." He paused and then smiled, like he was pleased with himself. "That's my big word for the day."

He moved from the back area toward the office area, and motioned for me to walk through the divider's swinging gate. He walked over and stood in front of one of the desks.

"This is *my* desk," he said, pointing at the desk in front of him. Then he pointed to another desk next to it. "That's *your* desk." He paused. "If I ever find your stuff on my desk, it goes in that can." He pointed at a wastepaper container next to his desk. "Understood?"

I nodded.

"And if you ever find *my* stuff on your desk, that means that I want you to take care of whatever it is. Understood?"

I nodded again.

"Now, let's sit down and see if your interviewing skills are what you say they are," he said, motioning to my desk chair.

I sat down, and then he sat down in a chair next to my desk.

"Now, you pretend that you are the reporter, and I'm the interviewee," he said, looking at me intently, like he was waiting for me to ask him a question. At that very moment, the boy walked up behind Rand, to ask him something. It was as though Rand had eyes in the back of his head, because, before a word could even come out of the boy's mouth, Rand picked up the folded newspaper, flipped around, and hit the boy over the head.

"Bug off. Can't you see I'm being interviewed?" Rand said. Then he turned back to me, leaned toward me, and said in a quiet voice, "That's John, my apprentice. Pay no attention to him."

He leaned back in his chair, and as he did, noticed the time on the clock on the opposite wall.

"Jesus, John. It's almost four o'clock," he yelled across the room. "Why didn't you tell me?"

"But that's what I was trying . . ."

"I'll take care of things here. You take Mr. Lovit and the equipment, and get up to the west bluff," he said, cutting the boy off.

Then Rand looked at me.

"We do a little photography on the side, just to supplement the business," he said almost apologetically. "I'm not real good with the flash powder," he added.

I realized I'd just been enlisted to do some photography. Rand seemed quite happy to find someone besides himself, that would get blown up if there was a problem with the flash powder. But *I* was happy just to have the job.

As John and I walked up Grand Hill, lugging the equipment, he filled me in on the assignment. We passed the Grand Hotel, and as soon as we started up the hill toward the bluff, I could see people gathering at the top of the hill.

I'll admit, that I was in sort of a daze. This all seemed like a dream to me. The air was so fresh, and the sky was so blue, and the water so glorious. I positioned the camera to get both the cottages and the west end of the Grand Hotel in the background. I had John position the six ladies, and then the one gentleman.

"Where's Kathleen?" one of the girls asked another.

At that same moment, I looked out from the hood of the camera and saw a beautiful young woman running down the stairs of the wedding cake house. She seemed to float down the stairs, and the light of her smile eclipsed the afternoon sunlight.

"I'm coming," she replied.

Her voice was musical, and I couldn't take my eyes off her.

As she walked toward me, our eyes met. She smiled kindly, but there was a deeper connection beyond the smile. Like she was my best friend in the whole world. Like I could tell her anything, and she would understand.

"Ok, let's all get in position," one of the ladies said in a bossy tone of voice.

Her abrupt tone brought my mind back to the task at hand.

"Ok, everyone hold perfectly still," I said, starting to put the hood over my head, finding it hard to take my eyes off of Kathleen.

"Perfectly still," came an echo from *Miss Bossy*.

I looked up, startled again by this obnoxious woman. Then I looked at Kathleen, and she smiled at me, and rolled her eyes.

I put my head under the hood, and looked through the lens. I almost passed out. I was dizzy, and my knees bowed, almost giving out.

"Dear, God. This is the picture," I said aloud.

"A good picture, Mr. Lovit?" I heard John ask, trying to confirm what I'd said underneath the hood.

"A marvelous picture, John."

I took my time taking the picture. I just sat there looking through the lens at her. I could look as long as I wanted, and no one would know I was staring at her, because I was shielded by the hood. But soon my euphoria was shattered.

"Are we almost done?" came a demanding voice from that same annoying woman.

"All right, everyone. Three, two, one."

Puff! And the picture was history.

## SIX

# Love of My Life

I stood there and watched Kathleen as she walked back to the wedding cake house with one of the other ladies. She looked back over her shoulder at me, and then quickly looked away.

John and I packed up the equipment and headed back down the hill to the Gazette. John had watched me intently while I was taking the photo, and I thought that maybe I could help spark his interest.

"So, John. Would you like me to teach you how to take photographs?"

John gave me a strange look. "Mr. Lovit, did you know that there are people in the Amazon that won't let you take their photograph? They believe that it will steal their souls."

"Yeah, I read that, John. Believe me, someday it *will* steal people's souls."

"What do you mean?"

"I mean that, someday, people won't think that they *have* a soul, unless they are photographed."

"That's strange, Mr. Lovit. *You're* strange. But I like you. You're ok."

"Thanks, John. You're ok too."

I felt like this was a good opportunity to ask John something that had been on my mind since that afternoon.

"So John. I was just wondering. Does it bother you when Rand hits you with the newspaper?"

"Oh, heck no. He'd never hurt a fly, especially me. If it wasn't for Rand, I'd have no family at all. He took me in when my parents died. Gave me my job. Takes me fishin'. No, he's just funnin' when he hits me with the paper. If he ever stopped doing it, I'd think something was wrong. He's the best friend I have in the whole world."

"That's what I thought. But I just thought I'd ask. So, you never did answer me. Do you want to learn how to take photographs?"

"I already know how, Mr. Lovit, but don't tell Rand. He'd want me to go all over the place taking photographs, and then we wouldn't have as much time for fishin'."

"Your secret is safe with me," I told him.

By this time, we had arrived back at the newspaper office. I looked inside through the screen door, but there was no one there. I turned around, and John had already started to walk on down the street.

"What time do we start work tomorrow?" I yelled to John.

"Oh, we don't do a paper on weekends. Not usually, anyway. And we don't do a paper when Rand doesn't want to. We just do it when he feels like it. Sometimes it's a morning paper, and sometimes an evening paper. But never a weekend paper. Well, almost, never, and . . ."

"Ok. Ok. I get the picture," I replied.

"*What* picture, Mr. Lovit?"

"It's just a saying, John. Or at least it *will* be."

"Hmm? See you Monday, Mr. Lovit."

"Aren't you going to lock up?" I yelled.

He just looked at me like I was out of my mind, and walked on down the street.

*   *   *

On Saturday morning, the first order of business was to deal with the exorbitant amount of currency I'd brought with me. I needed to hide it somewhere. And I decided if I converted it to gold, I could hide it without having to worry about water damage, or about some mouse or rat eating it. I went to the bank, not knowing what kind of reaction I would get to the amount of cash I was carrying, or the reaction I would get for exchanging it to gold.

Mr. Jackson, the bank's president, handled the transaction personally. And though he did express concern for my safety, and suggested that I put the gold in a safety deposit box, the exchange was all done matter-of-factly. I'm sure he hoped that sooner or later, I would deposit it back into his bank.

When I returned to the hotel room, I looked all around the room for a good hiding place for the bags of gold. I thought about hiding it in the furniture, but decided that would be too risky. I noticed a piece of loose baseboard, and tried pulling it away from the wall. It came off too easily.

If it came off so easily for me, someone else might notice that it was loose, also. So I stuffed the bags of gold way back under the floor boards, between the floor joists, and then put the baseboard back over the area. Then I moved my bed up against the baseboard, so that no one would notice it was loose. And even if they did notice it and remove the baseboard, the bags of gold were so far under the floorboards, that they couldn't see them, let alone reach them.

As I went to lunch that noon, I noticed a small poster hanging on the bulletin board in the lobby.

Join us for
*A Grand Benefit*
*for*
*The Park Project*
**Grand Hotel**
*Saturday, May 20th, 8 p.m.*

"What a fantastic opportunity to meet the woman of my dreams," I thought. I knew I had to go.

\* \* \*

It was around 8:15 as I walked into the Grand Hotel dining room. My heart was racing. I didn't know anyone, and I had no idea of where I would sit, or with whom. I only knew that *she* might be there, and I had to seize the opportunity.

I looked all around the room, looking for her, but she was nowhere to be found. Then I heard a voice from behind me.

"Mr. Lovit. Mr. Lovit."

I turned around, and there was Mr. Jackson, the bank president. He was seated at a round table, with a woman on his right (that I assumed to be his wife), two other couples, and an unescorted woman. I didn't recognize any of those with him.

"Whom are you looking for? Perhaps I can be of some assistance?" he asked.

"Oh, no. I just . . . I'm just looking for a place to sit," I replied.

"Won't you join us?" he asked.

"Oh, yes! Please join us," said the round, jolly woman on his right.

Mr. Jackson was a friendly gentleman in his mid-sixties. At first I thought he had asked me to join them in hopes that I would put my gold in his bank. But it didn't take too long to see that this man was truly warm and genuine.

"Mr. Lovit is from Kansas," Mr. Jackson announced to those seated at the table.

"Oh, how delightful. I don't think I've ever met anyone from Kansas," said a petite woman in her thirties, seated to Mr. Jackson's left.

Mr. Jackson began to make introductions.

"This is my wife," Mr. Jackson said, pointing to the woman on his right, the one I had suspected was his wife. "This is Mr. and Mrs. Lee," he said, pointing first to the petite woman who had *never met anyone from Kansas*, and then to her husband seated on her left. "This is Miss Bender," he said pointing to the unescorted woman on Mr. Lee's left. "And this is Mr. and Mrs. Peterson," he finished, pointing to a handsome young couple in their twenties, seated on the right of Mrs. Jackson.

"Please sit down," Mr. Jackson said.

I sat down in the empty chair, Mrs. Peterson at my left, and Miss Bender at my right.

"So where in Kansas are you from?" Mr. Lee asked inquisitively.

"Oh, a little town on the Oklahoma border. I'm sure you haven't heard of it."

"Southwest Kansas?" he asked without a pause.

"Yes," I said, hoping he wouldn't ask any more questions.

"I've been to Dodge City several times," he said in a questioning tone, as though he doubted my truthfulness.

I'd been to Dodge City when I was a child, and felt this was my opportunity to put the matter to rest, and shut this guy up.

"Yes, it's not too far from my hometown. We visited there many times when I was a child. Visited the graveyard where . . ." I was going to say, 'the graveyard where all those outlaws that Wyatt Earp *supposedly* killed were buried.' But he cut me off, and it was a good thing he did.

"Yes, all those outlaws Wyatt Earp killed." And then he went on offering a complete chronology of the Kansas lawman. I knew my history about Earp. He had only killed one man in all his days. But the legend of the day was obviously bigger than history. And I knew I shouldn't say any more.

"Did you ever meet Wyatt Earp?" Mrs. Peterson asked.

"Ah, no. I think he had moved on to Tombstone by then," I answered, hoping we could change the subject.

"Oh, how exciting," Mrs. Jackson offered. "Wyatt Earp. Outlaws. And Tombstone!"

"Oh, look who's here," Mrs. Peterson said, motioning toward a table across the room. I was relieved the subject had changed. But I was *ecstatic* to see who the new subject was. *Kathleen!*

She had on a striking emerald green dress, her dark hair was up, and she looked — *angelic* is the only word that even comes close to describing her appearance. She was smiling, but underneath the smile, I sensed a deep sadness. A man in military dress uniform was seating her.

"Oh, and Captain Sallee is with her," said Mrs. Lee.

"I thought the Captain was in Chicago," said Mrs. Jackson.

Miss Bender piped in. "He just got back today. You can always tell when he's back. Kathleen's smile dims considerably."

I looked across the room at Kathleen, and then at her father, the Captain. He seemed like such a stern man, and I wondered how such a lovely and kind human being as Kathleen could have come out of his loins. I wanted to ask questions about her, but I knew it would be indecorous. I hoped that the conversation would eventually come back around to Kathleen, so I could learn more about her.

There was a small orchestra playing during dinner, and after dinner, couples began to take to the dance floor. They looked so elegant. And watching them dance made me thankful that my mother had taken the time to teach me to dance.

I sat there for nearly an hour, trying to get the nerve to ask Kathleen to dance. But as the evening progressed, I noticed she hadn't danced with anyone the entire evening, and that the Captain seemed to be standing watch over her. I gave up hope of asking her to dance, but I couldn't help but steal a glance, whenever I could. She didn't look at me. But I could tell she knew I was watching her.

I slowly tuned out the conversations at the table, and began to daydream about spending a day with Kathleen, walking on the beach in the bright sunlight. I was almost in a dream state, when I heard something that brought me back to reality and to the conversation at the table.

"Oh, yes. That was when Sir Reginald visited the island. He was in *Love of My Life*, at the opera house," I heard Mrs. Jackson say.

"*Love of My Life*? I know that play. We put on a musical version of it at my school. It's one of my favorites," I said.

"Why that's wonderful," Mrs. Lee said. "You should do a rendition of it here on the island."

Mrs. Peterson piped in. "Oh, yes. What a wonderful idea. We have so many talented people here on the island this summer. I'm sure they would love to be involved." Then she looked at me very seriously. "But a word of warning, Mr. Lovit. Matty Johnson. She won't be very pleased with the idea, unless she's involved."

I could see everyone at the table nod in agreement.

"Involved? Ha! You mean, unless she is the dictator," Miss Bender added.

"Really?" I asked, wondering who this person was.

"Oh, yes. *Really*. You'll find out soon enough who she is. She had a small part in the play when Sir Reginald was here, and now she thinks she owns the play," said Miss Bender.

"Now, dear. We shouldn't be talking about her behind her back. She's a nice lady," said Mrs. Jackson.

"To your face, maybe," said Mrs. Peterson, rebutting Mrs. Jackson. Then Mrs. Peterson leaned toward me until her face was directly in front of mine. "Watch your back, Mr. Lovit. She'll put a knife in it."

"Dear!" Mr. Peterson said to his wife.

"Well, no one likes her. She claims to be friends with Sir Reginald, and I know for a fact that he can't stand her," Mrs. Peterson added.

"I think we should dance, dear," Mr. Peterson said to his wife, grabbing her by the hand, and escorting her to the dance floor.

"I'm sorry, Mr. Lovit. But Matty Johnson has a way of being the center of attention, even when she isn't in the room," said Mrs. Jackson.

I looked around the table, and watched the eyes roll in consensus. And then Miss Bender gave me a physical description of this *Matty* person, and I realized that I'd met her. She was the obnoxious woman from the photo I'd taken the day before.

"This is a marvelous idea, Mr. Lovit," said Mrs. Lee, bringing the subject back to the play. "Kathleen Sallee is a wonderful actress, and she has a beautiful voice."

I couldn't believe it. It was too good to be true.

"And I have done set designs for a number of our productions here. I'd be so very happy to help," Mrs. Lee finished.

"I'll give it some serious thought. Very serious," I said. "Well, I really must be going. It's been a very pleasant and enlightening evening."

I said my goodbyes to everyone at the table, and waved and smiled across the dance floor to Mr. and Mrs. Peterson. Kathleen's father was having a very merry time on the dance floor with the ladies, and I assumed from how merry a time he was having, that he must be a widower.

I turned to go, and looked toward the table where Kathleen was sitting, hoping to catch one last glance before leaving. She was nowhere to be seen.

\* \* \*

Sunday morning I went to the little Stone Church, because I thought *she* might be there. She was there, but again, with her father. And again, he hovered over her like he had the night before.

\* \* \*

It was Monday morning, May 22nd, 1905, and I awoke bright and early. I had a huge breakfast, and headed out the door of the hotel, toward the newspaper.

I was on top of the world. The sun was shining, and the water and sky was that color of blue that you only see on Mackinac. The air was cool and fresh, the birds were singing, and, most importantly, I was in love.

All Sunday evening I'd been thinking about the play. Of course, it would be a wonderful way to meet her, and to get to know her. But besides that, I was really excited about the idea of producing the play. Not that I was a producer. But there had been many versions of *Love of My Life* done since 1905, on stage, and even on film. And I had seen many of them. I had the advantage of knowing many of the variations, and over the years, I had even thought of some additional musical numbers that I felt would fit nicely.

When I got to the Gazette, Rand was sitting in his chair, his feet up on his desk, and he was smoking a cigar. The smoke filled the office.

"No paper today, Lovit."

"No paper?"

"No news. Got to have some news to have a paper. Just the way it goes here."

I began to see what John was talking about, when he said that Rand did a paper whenever he felt like it.

"What's John up to?" I asked.

"He's down on the dock, getting the boat ready to go. We're gonna do some fishing. You can go too if you'd like. I've got a beautiful little Mackinac boat down on the dock, and she's just a waitin'."

I thought this would be the perfect opportunity to begin organizing the play. I had my desk, and peace and quiet.

"I think I'll just hang around here."

"Have you ever been fishing on the Great Lakes, Lovit? There's nothing like it in the whole wide world. It's not like those little mud holes you have back in Kansas," he laughed, deriding my home state.

On his desk was a pail with two bottles of drink, a couple of sandwiches, and several sticks of dynamite. He saw me looking at the dynamite.

"Oh, don't tell anyone. I'm trying to inculcate some new methods of fishing into my repertoire. That's two big words for the day. Sure you don't want to go?"

He inhaled deeply from his cigar, and the end of it glowed brightly.

"Are you sure you ought to be smoking around that stuff?" I asked him, taking a couple of steps back from the dynamite.

"You worry too much. You need to relax. Why don't you go fishing with us today?"

"I'll take you up on the offer some other time. I've just got some stuff I really want to work on."

"No problem. What are you working on?"

"I'm going to produce a play. Someone at the Park Benefit Dinner at the Grand Hotel on Saturday suggested it. I think I'll really enjoy it. Do you know any of the local talent around here?"

"A few. Why don't you put an ad in the next paper we run? You could even print up some posters. Oh, and put something up at the opera house."

"Hey, that's a great idea. Thanks."

"And what are you in such a cheery mood about this morning?"

"It shows?"

"You come in here singing, a smile on your face. If I didn't know better, I'd say you were in love. But then, you haven't been here long enough to meet anyone."

I didn't say a word.

"Ah, you *are* in love. Met her at the Grand on Saturday night, didn't you?" he asked.

"Yes."

"And does she like you back?"

"Well, I haven't actually spoken to her. Yet. Her father was standing guard over her all night. I couldn't even get within ten yards of her."

"And who, might I ask, is this fair lady?"

"Captain Sallee's daughter. Kathleen."

Rand choked on his cigar, and he almost fell out of his chair.

"Are you out of your mind, man? She's not his daughter. Kathleen is his *wife!*"

\*　　\*　　\*

The next thing I remembered was the smell of ammonia stinging my nostrils, and the patterns of the tin ceiling, and Rand on his knees beside me, looking down at me.

"Are you all right, man?"

I had passed out, and *why* I'd passed out came back to me very quickly. Captain Sallee, the Great Lakes captain, the wedding cake house, his murder, and most of all, his murderer — the photographer of the photo — me!

Why I hadn't put it all together before then I don't know. But I finally did put it together. And it hit me like a ton of bricks.

"Oh, geez. Just my luck. I travel seventy years to be with a woman, and she's married," I said aloud.

"Lovit. You better get to a doctor. You hit your head pretty hard."

"I'm fine."

"No, you're not fine. You're talking gibberish."

"I'll be all right. Guess I'm just shocked, that's all."

"Let me give you a word of advice. Stay away from Kathleen. Captain Sallee is no man to be trifled with."

With that, the front screen door opened. Rand looked up, and then back down at me.

"Speak of the devil," he said out of the side of his mouth. Rand got off his knees and onto his feet.

"Captain Sallee. How are you, sir?" he said to the man that had just entered the door.

By this time the Captain was standing over me, looking down. His look was not one of concern, but of disgust.

"My man just had somewhat of a fall. I'm sure he'll be all right," Rand tried to explain.

Rand helped me to my chair.

"I need to place an ad in your paper," the Captain said demandingly.

"Yes, sir."

"Take a note."

"Yes, sir."

"Wanted: Able bodied, experienced seaman, to assist with ship and dock duties, moving heavy equipment from Chicago to Detroit. Length of duty from June 15$^{th}$ to August 15$^{th}$. Please report to dock office between June 1$^{st}$ and June 14$^{th}$."

"Is that it, sir?"

"I want it in starting tomorrow. I want it to run every day until the 14$^{th}$ of June."

Then he turned and walked out the door, without even saying goodbye.

"Is he always that demanding?" I asked Rand.

"He thinks he's captain of this whole damned island."

"He must have *some* redeeming qualities, being married to someone as wonderful as Kathleen."

"Yeah, omnipotent arrogance," he said sarcastically. "That's four big words for the day. That's gotta be a record for me."

Then he went on to give me the scoop on the Captain. "Let me tell you something. That man is a son of a bitch. That's what he is, Lovit. Kathleen is the kindest person you'll ever meet, and I've seen her more than once with a black eye, or with bruises. She always says she fell off her horse, but everyone on this island knows better."

If the man had still been in the room, I would have killed him then and there.

"And let me tell you another thing, man. He had a deck-hand on his ship that was givin' Kathleen a bit too much of the eye. And when the ship was on the leg back from Chicago, that fellow just happened to fall overboard, and drowned. That's just too much of a coincidence for me."

I began reading the ad that the Captain had dictated to Rand. Rand looked at me suspiciously.

"I know what you're thinking, Lovit. You're out of your mind, man. You are out of your mind."

## SEVEN
# Auditions

I was pretty out of sorts for several days. I couldn't believe that she was married. And there were so many things I didn't understand. Would I be the one to kill the Captain? Maybe he wouldn't be killed at all. Certainly time events could be changed. I had the choice to kill him. And as much as I wanted to kill him, after I learned of the way he treated Kathleen, I felt there had to be another solution. There had to be some other way to help her out of the situation.

The Captain would be gone from the 15th of June until the 15th of August. I hoped that I could find a way to see her, and somehow, convince her to get away from him. Maybe even take her back to 1975, and we could live *happily ever after*.

At any rate, there was nothing I could do about it until he left. So, the next week was spent pulling things together for the play. I arranged with the opera house to do performances from Tuesday, August 8th, through Saturday, August 12th. On May 31st, I put an advertisement in the paper, to try and bring the talent together. The first response I received was quite interesting:

*June 1, 1905*

*Dear Mr. Lovit:*

*I am writing this letter to let you know of my extreme disapproval of your decision to produce LOVE OF MY LIFE.*

*I personally know, and am very close friends with, the writer, and intend to let him know of your intentions. LOVE OF MY LIFE, was inspired by God Himself, and for anyone to have the audacity to think that they could do a production that would even come close to the glory, and splendor, and holiness of the original, is sacrilege.*

*I will do everything in my power (and God Almighty Himself will help me) to stop you from profaning the memory of LOVE OF MY LIFE.*

*Matty B. Johnson*

I'd been warned about this Matty character, and now I understood what everyone was trying to tell me about. I guess I might have been more upset, had I not been forewarned about her, and had it not been for the second response I received:

*June 1, 1905*

*Dear Mr. Lovit,*

*I was so thrilled to hear about your production of* <u>*Love of My Life*</u>. *I have always loved the story, but have always felt that it was incomplete, somehow. I was thrilled to read in your article in the Gazette that you felt the same way.*

*I would love to be involved in anyway possible. I could help with painting sets, costumes, or refreshments. I am at your disposal from June 15th, through August 14th. Please send all correspondence to:*

*K. Sallee, Grand Hotel, Island*

*It is very important that all correspondence to me be sent to the Grand Hotel. Thank you for your consideration.*

*Sincerely,*

*Kathleen Sallee*

*P.S. I can sing and act a little too, in case you need an extra, or maybe even an understudy (smile).*

I couldn't believe it. She wanted to be involved in the play. Everyone at the Park Benefit Dinner had raved about her singing ability. Yet she was so self-effacing. What a contrast to the letter I'd received from Matty Johnson.

It was too good to be true. It was the perfect opportunity to get to know her. I fired off a response immediately. My response was businesslike, but very open ended. A real *please-tell-me-more-about-yourself* kind of letter.

* * *

The next two weeks were completely hectic. Trying to do my job. Trying to put things together for the play. And all of this while trying to acclimatize myself to living in 1905. It was more difficult than I had possibly imagined. It was like living in a foreign country. And I soon learned that my speech was filled with more idiomatic phrases from 1975 than I had realized, and that my whole approach to life was a 1975 approach.

But over those two weeks came the greatest consolation. Letters from Kathleen. One nearly every day. And my delight was to write her back, which I would do every night in my hotel room, at around 2 a.m. I never felt tired. I never ran out of things to say. And what was really amazing was, I didn't feel separated from her. I felt like we were in the same house, and she was just in the next room. I had never even spoken to the woman in person, but I already felt like she was my best friend.

At first, the letters were all about the play, but then we began to write about everything under the sun. And I couldn't believe how alike we were. I felt I could tell her anything, and it would be safe with her.

I hoped that the letters would be for her eyes only, and I had assumed that was why she had asked me to write her at the Grand Hotel. I knew she must have friends there that empathized with her, and knew of the Captain's cruelty to her.

*    *    *

On the morning of June 15th, I left the hotel for work, and saw the Captain's ship heading out of port. I felt relieved. He was finally gone, and would *be* gone, until after the play was over. I could finally see Kathleen.

When I arrived at the Gazette, Rand was sitting behind his desk, smoking his breakfast cigar. There was nothing to do. But I sat at my desk, and pretended to work, while organizing more details of the play.

"So how's the play coming along?" Rand asked.

"It's coming. I've gotten quite a few letters from people who want to be involved."

"Have you heard anything from the infamous Matty snake-in-the-grass?"

"You mean, Matty Johnson?"

"Yep."

"As a matter of fact, hers was the first letter I received."

"Big surprise. Real supportive, I'll bet," Rand said sarcastically.

"How did you know?"

"She's a real piece of work. You really jumped into a pit of vipers when you decided to do that play."

"Hers was the only negative letter I got."

"Yeah, well, now you know what the *B.* stands for in *Matty B. Johnson*. Her whole life is that play. She'll fight you tooth and nail. And she'll get the Captain involved too."

"Captain Sallee?"

"You bet your life. She's his . . . you know."

"What do you mean?"

"You know. He's got one in every port. She's his here on the island."

"That son of a bitch. How could he do that to Kathleen?"

"He does pretty much whatever he wants, to *whomever* he wants. I told you before, he's not a man to be trifled with. And he and Matty make a perfect couple."

"He doesn't deserve someone like Kathleen," I scowled.

"No one deserves Kathleen, Lovit. She's an angel. Everyone on this island will tell you that. Oh, speaking of Kathleen." He reached into his vest pocket and handed me a letter on familiar stationery. "You got another letter from her."

I took the letter, sat down at my desk, and began reading it. And as always, the sweetness of her words made me smile from ear to ear. Rand saw me smiling.

"Here, let me read that," he said. He grabbed the letter out of my hands, and walked around to the front of my desk.

I reached over the desk and tried to grab the letter back from him. But he backed out of my reach, and then started to read it aloud.

"Hello, Hello," he said, reading the first two words she had written. Then his face lit up, and he began to dance around my desk, singing the words over and over. He put the letter to his nose, and breathed deeply, then put the letter under my nose, teasing me. "Oh, and it's perfumed too. Smells just like the lilacs bloomin' all over this island."

"Hello, hello. Yeah, so what? Perfume. So what?" I said, trying to ignore his adolescent taunts.

"*You* know, Lovit. The song from that musical. *Hello, Hello. Can't you see that I'm falling in love with you? That* song."

"What in the hell are you talking about?"

"Don't you know an ellipsis when you see one? You daft boy. She should be in love with someone a damned sight smarter than you. Hey! *Ellipsis*. That's my big word for the day"

"In love? With me? You're crazy," I said.

"Oh, God, Lovit. You *are* daft."

\*　　\*　　\*

It was Saturday, June 17<sup>th</sup>. Waiting so long to do the auditions, had left only seven weeks for rehearsals. But I had to wait until the Captain left the island. I had to make sure Kathleen could audition.

I was amazed at how many people showed up that evening for the auditions. And even more amazed at how much talent there was on the island. It seemed like everyone could do something. And I couldn't help but think of how television had robbed people of artistic initiative in my day and time. I tried to remember who had invented television, and just for a moment, entertained the idea of finding him, and trying to persuade him to a different career.

I wanted to work with talented people. But more importantly, I wanted to work with people who could be worked with. And the amount of talent of those auditioning seemed to be in reverse proportion to the bragging on their resumes. I was able to discern very quickly between the humble and the egotist, and it made my choice much simpler.

One young man in particular, Paul Martin, was fantastic for the leading role. Paul was a natural actor, a singer, and a fine musician. We had so many things in common, and we hit it off right away.

Not all of the people were so talented. One woman had a voice that sounded like a five-year-old practicing the violin. I endured her screeching, only because Kathleen still had not arrived.

"Does anyone know where Kathleen Sallee is?" I shouted over the din.

The woman stopped right in the middle of her note, and stalked off the stage, thoroughly offended by my rudeness. I know I was rude, but I'd reached my saturation point with the noise, and with the anxiety that Kathleen might not show for the audition.

"Anyone?" I repeated quietly.

I had no more than said the words, when Kathleen appeared on the stage. The whole room hushed. They knew something I would soon find out. She took her place. The accompanist began to play.

And she began to sing. Dear God! She was captivating.

I was in love with her. The whole room was in love with her. It wasn't just good singing, or talent. It was much more than that. It was *her*. She radiated gentleness and kindness. Goodness. I don't know how to describe it. But I knew I'd found my leading lady — for life.

I couldn't tell you how long the song was. Time disappeared. I glanced to one end of the stage, and saw Paul Martin gazing at her with admiration. I could tell from the way he looked at her, that a love of music was not the only thing we shared. He was obviously in love with her too.

She finished her song, and the only sounds I heard were people sniffling, or blowing their noses.

She walked down the steps on the left side of the stage, and began to talk with Paul. I walked toward the stage, and my legs felt numb, like they didn't want to move. Like in a dream, when you're trying to run away from someone, and your legs just won't work. My heart was racing. And even though we'd been writing to each other for the last two weeks, for some reason, I suddenly felt self-conscious and awkward in her presence.

I became acutely aware that I was from another time. I was starting to become acclimated to this world. But now, meeting her, the woman in the picture; the picture that I'd seen that first day I'd arrived on Mackinac Island; the picture that I'd taken the first day I'd arrived to live here in the past . . . it was all too much for me. I didn't know how to act. I didn't know what to say.

"Marvelous. Marvelous! Unbelievable. There are no words to describe," I said, stumbling on my words, and practically stumbling down the aisle.

I felt embarrassed at my effusiveness. My face turned red, and I felt like I had *I love you* written all over my face. Kathleen began to blush, and I didn't know if I'd embarrassed her, or if she was simply embarrassed for *me*.

"It was good seeing you, Mrs. Sallee," Paul said to her. And then he looked at me. "So you'll be letting us know, soon?"

"Letting you know? Oh, about the part. You definitely have the part. But please don't mention it to anyone, yet. I'll be sending out letters in a day or two. It's just a formality. And you too, Mrs. Sallee. You have the part," I said, still stumbling on my words.

Paul grinned broadly, but he wasn't looking at me. He was looking at Kathleen, and I realized why. Because in the play, his character gets to kiss Kathleen's character. At that moment, I would have wished that I were an actor, instead of the producer. Only, Kathleen wasn't looking at him, or smiling at him. Her eyes were fixed on me, and she wouldn't stop smiling.

"So, goodbye, Mrs. Sallee," Paul said.

"Goodbye, Mr. Martin," she said. But her eyes never left mine.

It seemed almost out of character for her. From what I'd heard and seen, she was never inconsiderate to anyone. And I would have felt sorry for him, but, she was looking at me. And I was lost in her eyes.

"I want to thank you, Mr. Lovit, for allowing me to audition for this play."

I had only heard her speak once before — that day I took the photograph. And I had just heard her sing. But now, for the first time, she spoke to me. And her voice was just as beautiful as when she was singing. It was music. It was soft and warm. Not too high. Not too low. Very, very, feminine. And she had the most delightful Irish lilt.

I couldn't speak. I tried, but nothing would come out of my mouth.

"Are you ready to go?" I heard a voice say from behind us.

"Pleasant evening, Mr. Lovit," she said with a smile. But she looked slightly puzzled, being perplexed by my silence. And then she walked away. All I could do was stand there.

\*　　\*　　\*

It only took a couple of days to put together the list of principals and understudies. We met for the first time on Monday, June 19th, and decided to rehearse twice a week: on Monday afternoons and Saturday evenings. It wasn't a lot of time to rehearse, so I counted on everyone to study as much as they could on their own. And I was amazed at how quickly things progressed.

Kathleen and I said very little to each other publically. But privately, we continued to write each other every day. I didn't know it was possible to become so close to someone by letters. But Kathleen and I were *cut from the same cloth* (as she put it), and at rehearsals, it only took a glance to communicate our feelings.

I didn't see any way that we could ever see each other outside of rehearsals, but at the end of our rehearsal on Monday afternoon, July 3$^{rd}$, Kathleen approached me.

"Mr. Lovit. Some of us are going over to the Murphy for dinner, and I thought that you might care to join us?"

"I would love to."

"At seven?" she asked.

"At seven," I answered, smiling.

\* \* \*

When I arrived at the Murphy, Kathleen was standing on the sidewalk with a pretty, dark-haired woman, and a gentleman that I presumed to be her husband. I had assumed that some of the other cast and crew would be there, and had actually hoped they would be, for propriety's sake. But there was no one else.

"Where are the others?" I asked.

"Mr. Lovit, I would like you to meet Mr. Ezekiel Browning, and his wife, Mary Browning. They are my dearest friends," Kathleen said, without answering my question. I immediately understood that there was never anyone else coming. That these people were her trusted friends.

We all went into the restaurant and were seated at a booth. Ezekiel and I were seated on one side, Ezekiel on the inside. Kathleen and Mary were seated on the other side, Mary on the inside. We ordered our food, and began to make conversation.

It was easy to see that Ezekiel and his wife absolutely adored each other. And they were both very easy to get along with. I gleaned from my conversation with Ezekiel, that he owned a hotel somewhere, and I was pretty sure that it was here on the island. But every time I brought it up, he would change the subject. Yet, he talked unreservedly about everything else under the sun. Especially their children, which seemed to be the favorite topic of the evening.

Kathleen and Mary were giggling like school girls, and were quite obviously best friends. At one point, they got into a discussion about using one's first names (or *Christian* names, as they referred to them) in public, and asked me what I thought of it. Of all the 1975 habits that I'd had to break since arriving here, using one's first name in public situations was probably the hardest to break. I had seriously offended several people on several occasions, and realized the importance inculcating this protocol into my life. And I still hadn't been able to figure out when it *was* right to use them, so I probably sounded too formal.

"I think it's silly not to be able to address people by their Christian names in public," said Kathleen.

"I would never think of doing that," Mary rebutted.

"I think protocol is a wonderful way of showing respect for others," I said.

"Very well put, Mr. Lovit. A code we live by, for the purpose of showing respect and kindness to others," Ezekiel said.

"But an appropriate departure from the rule can sometimes show tremendous respect, don't you agree, Mr. Lovit?" Kathleen asked rhetorically, looking at me with affection.

"But how do you determine if it is an appropriate departure?" Mary asked.

"If it performs the intent of the rule, which is to show respect and kindness," I stated, still looking at Kathleen.

"Again, very well put, Mr. Lovit. I've met many people who use rules and laws for the exact opposite of the purpose for which they were intended. And they invariably do it for their own gain," Ezekiel added.

"Well, we certainly know someone like that, don't we?" Mary said, looking at Kathleen.

Kathleen started to answer, "You mean . . . ?"

"It's a lovely evening, dear. Lets talk about something pleasant," Ezekiel said to Mary.

"Wonderful idea," Kathleen added.

Kathleen did indeed change the subject, but I couldn't, for the life of me, tell you what she said after that point. Here before me was the loveliest, kindest, most intelligent woman that I had ever met, but I couldn't hear a word she was saying. I just wanted to bask in the warm glow of her visage, and in the soothing tone of her voice.

We stayed for nearly two hours, and it was a wonderful evening. Then I started to get up out of the booth, and was about halfway up when, I felt an incredibly strong sense of déjá vu. The sights and sounds were so familiar to me. I realized that this was what I'd seen in the flashback, that first day I'd come to Mackinac Island. The carpet. And Kathleen, in her dress, and the necklace. And then I suddenly remembered I was from 1975, and 1975 didn't seem real to me. 1905 was becoming my reality, and I'd become so accustomed to it, that I began to doubt my own sanity. Doubt whether or not I *was* from 1975. I almost passed out.

"Are you all right, Mr. Lovit?" Ezekiel asked me.

"I think so. I must have gotten up too fast," I answered him. But I knew that wasn't it at all.

We walked out of the restaurant, into the hallway. A young bellhop walked past us with a stack of dishes. And suddenly, he dropped them. Pieces flew everywhere, and the manager started yelling at him. People started laughing at the boy. And I remembered seeing this exact incident in the flashback that I'd had that first day I'd arrived on Mackinac.

"I can't believe the way some people treat their help," Ezekiel said as we walked to the front doors.

"And people laughing at that poor boy! How cruel," said Mary.

We walked out the front doors of the Murphy, and their carriage was waiting.

"So you're staying here at the Murphy, right Mr. Lovit?" Mary asked me. I took the hint, that I should say goodnight. But Kathleen changed that plan.

"Mr. Lovit, would you be so kind as to accompany me on the ride home?" she asked.

"My pleasure," I said.

I was uncomfortable, not knowing what Ezekiel and Mary might have thought. But still, I was so glad Kathleen had asked me.

We all continued to chat as we rode up Grand Hill, and I could see why Kathleen considered them her friends. They were warm and friendly, very down-to-earth, and yet, they carried themselves with dignity and grace.

We pulled up in front of the Grand Hotel, and the carriage stopped.

"Oh, you're staying at the Grand?" I asked.

"You might say that," Ezekiel replied.

Mary interrupted. "It was a delightful evening. We must do it again sometime."

We said our goodnights, and the carriage continued up the hill toward Kathleen's house.

"I don't know why, but I never got to ask your friends where they were from. I just assumed they were from the island."

"They are."

"Oh, and they're staying at the Grand Hotel?"

"They live there, Mr. Lovit. Mr. Browning is the president of the hotel."

"I had no idea. Such nice people. Not at all pretentious. So unassuming."

"They want people to like them for *who* they are, not *what* they are, By the grace of God, I think that I have the most wonderful friends in the world," she said.

The carriage pulled up in front of the wedding cake house.

"And now I have another one," she said to me.

"Another one?"

"Another wonderful friend. Would you mind walking me to the door, my friend?"

I could tell she had something else she wanted to tell me. I got out on the left side of the carriage, walked around to the right side, and helped her down. I told the driver that I would walk home. Then Kathleen and I walked up her steps, and onto the porch.

"Have you seen much of the island since you arrived, Mr. Lovit?"

"Not really. I've been so busy with work and the play, that I really haven't had time."

"I'd like to show you around the island. Are you free tomorrow?" she asked.

I knew this was very forward for a lady of her era, not even to mention the fact that she was a married woman. I wanted more than anything in the world to spend time with her, but I found myself caring about her. Caring about her more than my own desires.

"But it's the 4th of July. Certainly you want to spend the holiday with your family?"

"The Captain is away, and I have no other living relatives here on the island. I have friends that

I could spend the day with, but I'd like to spend the day with *you*, Mr. Lovit."

"But, Mrs. Sallee. I don't want to do anything to damage your good name."

"My good name? I have the Captain's name. As you may have gleaned by now, it is a powerful name, but not a *good* one. As for my reputation, I don't care what people say anymore. I'm tired of waiting for my life to begin. I want my life to begin now, or I want to have no life at all."

I could tell she was absolutely serious.

"Our stables are behind the house. Meet me there at eight o'clock tomorrow morning, and we will go riding. You do ride?"

"When I was young. But I haven't ridden for years."

"At eight o'clock then?"

"I would love to, Mrs. Sallee."

"My name is Kathleen. Please call me Kathleen."

It was the way she said it. Like she felt liberated in saying it. It stirred my soul.

## EIGHT

# Independence Day

I wasn't a second late getting to the stables the next morning. Kathleen was already there, getting the horses ready. She smiled as I arrived, but I could tell she was uncomfortable. This was a big step for her, being with me, in front of God and everyone, and I could see the apprehension in her eyes. But I could also tell that this was something she had to do, and there was nothing that anyone could say to talk her out of it.

I had no idea where this was going for us. But I could tell that she was breaking away from the Captain, mentally. And though I was glad to be a catalyst in the situation, I hoped that wasn't all I was.

"David, could you hand me that bridle?"

She called me by my first name, and it felt so nice hearing her say my name.

"David," she said as she took the bridle. "That's a beautiful name."

"*Kathleen. That's* a beautiful name. I find myself walking around just saying it, just so I can hear it."

"I like hearing you say it," she said, smiling warmly. Then she swung up on her horse. "Are you ready to go?"

"Go? What do I do?"

"You rode when you were young. You just have to hop on, and go. It will all come back to you."

I mounted the horse, and we headed up the trail, behind the Grand Hotel, up toward Skull Cave.

"I heard you say last night at dinner that you are a schoolteacher."

"Right."

"Where is the school?"

"It's the white building, down by the potato field, in front of the fort."

"Oh. By Marquette Park?" I let slip.

"Our committee just got approval to turn the potato field into a park, and we *have* considered naming it Marquette Park, after Father Marquette. But how did you know that?"

"I . . . I . . . someone said."

"Well, someone's been talking too much. Anyway, the school is the white building."

"I thought that was the Indian Dormitory."

"It was built so the visiting Indians would have a place to stay, but they never used it. They didn't like to be inside. So the city turned it into a school in 1870. I went to school there as a child. You know quite a bit about the island, for having been here such a short time."

"Do you like teaching?" I asked, changing the subject.

"I couldn't live, if I couldn't teach. I love to see the face of a child light up when he or she really understands something. When they finally get it. It's the most wonderful feeling in the world."

"I hated school. But I'm sure I would have loved it, if I'd had you for a teacher."

"You seem so accomplished. You work for the paper. You are a photographer. And you're involved in the theater. You must have liked *some* parts of school."

"Yeah. The parts I liked, I liked. I loved music. That's why I became a musician."

"You're a musician? I play the violin. I love the violin, almost as much as I love horses. Whose music do you like?"

"I love Rachmaninoff. Rachmaninoff, Mahler, and Debussy are my favorites."

"Oh, yes, Rachmaninoff. The young man does show a lot of promise. Debussy is probably my favorite. And Mahler too."

"I love his 9th and 10th symphonies. Don't you?"

"He's only written *five* symphonies."

"I meant the 4th and 5th," I said matter-of-factly, remembering that six through ten hadn't been written yet. I suddenly realized how unsure I was about what I could talk about. And I wished that I'd studied harder in school; in music history and history in general.

"Do you like to read?" she asked. I was glad she'd changed the subject, but I came close to putting my foot right back in my mouth again.

"Some. I like movies better."

Too late, I'd already said it.

"Oh, wonderful. We have an Edison Kinetoscope, right downtown. Have you been there yet?"

"No."

I wanted to change the subject again; get back to something I was sure was already in existence. But I realized that I was beginning to sound rather guarded, like I was trying to hide something from her.

I wanted to talk openly with her. Explore each others hearts, the way we had in our letters. Even the night before, in the presence of Ezekiel and Mary, we had been comfortable. But now, being in each other's presence, alone together, we seemed almost like different people. Unable to open up. Uncomfortable.

"What about Shakespeare? Do you like romance?"

"I love romance." She paused. "But I hate tragedy. Romeo and Juliet. Tragedies are for people who can't feel anymore. I can feel. Everything. I want to be happy, and I want others to be happy. What's so wonderful about dying at 16? I don't ever want to die. But if I have to, I want to be happy, and healthy, and eighty-eight."

"Eighty-eight?" I wondered why she had chosen that number.

"Eight is my lucky number."

"I'll bet you'll live to be a hundred."

"I want to live forever. But if I make it to eighty-eight, I think I will have accomplished everything that I want to on this earth."

Then she looked at me mischievously, and said, "I'll bet you a penny to a cookie that I can beat you to Skull Cave."

"You're on," I said, knowing full well she'd win the race.

She dug in with her heels, and with a chick-chick sound, she was off. Visions of myself lying on the ground with broken bones and bloody body parts flashed through my mind. I don't know what got into me, but with a chick-chick, and a dig of my heels, I was off too. And I must say, I came in only a minute or two behind her.

We dismounted our horses, tied them to a post, and sat in the shade of a nearby tree.

"I'll bet you a penny to a cookie that you'll live to a hundred," I said, trying to catch my breath.

"You're on," she replied. "But you'd better be around to collect your cookie."

I looked into her eyes, and could see the emphasis of her words, was not on collecting the cookie, but on my being around.

We sat there, silently, for quite a while. And then I thought about something she had said earlier.

"What did you mean by tragedies are for people that can't feel anymore?" I asked her.

"I just feel like people in our day and time are becoming more and more spoiled. Almost scorched. Like they can't feel anymore, so they have to have more, and more, and more, to register any effect."

"If you think they are scorched now, wait for another seventy years," I said without thinking.

"Yes, I suppose that will be true. But why can't we appreciate the delicate, the subtle, the lovely, now, before it's all gone?"

It was at that moment, that I realized what a special gem she was. I felt so privileged that I'd been allowed to know her, if only for a short time.

"You are truly a special soul, Katie. If this world survives, it will be because of people like you."

"*Katie*? My father called me that. He is the only person who *ever* called me by that name. Why did you call me that?" she asked solemnly. She got up and walked over to the side of the cave.

"It just seemed to fit the wild horsewoman," I said, laughing.

"Do you know why they call it Skull Cave?" she asked me, abruptly changing the subject.

"Used to be an Indian burial place, right?"

"I'll have to get you into one of my classes," she said smiling.

I had thought for quite a while about whether or not I would show her, show anyone, the portal that had brought me to this time. But I was dying to tell her. Tell her where I was from, and how I'd gotten here.

"I have to show you something," I said, motioning her to the back side of the rocks. "Look!"

"Look at what?" she answered, puzzled. She walked to the stone wall, and ran her hands over the face, as if the opening wasn't there. "What am I supposed to see?"

I could tell she couldn't see the opening, but I didn't know *why*. I was tempted to walk forward into the opening. Disappear before her very sight. And then tell her the secret of the time portal. But I had complicated things too much already. Said way too much.

"Oh, nothing. Just thought you would enjoy the rock formations."

We started walking back down the trail, leading the horses behind us.

As much as I wanted to deny it, I was painfully aware of the fact that I was with a married woman. And even though she was making the break mentally from the Captain, sooner or later the horse dung (to put it in the 1905 vernacular) was going to hit the fan.

"So how did you end up with the Captain?" I asked her.

"Oh, that's a very long story."

"I'm not going anywhere."

She looked pensively down the road ahead of us, and she was silent so long, that I wasn't sure if she would open up. But finally, she let out a deep sigh, and began to speak.

"My grandfather made his fortune in the fur trade here on the island, and then lost everything when the trade declined in the 40's. He tried to make a go of it in fishing, but never really recovered. My father was born into the fishing trade, and made a better go of it than my grandfather. But he made some bad business decisions, and eventually lost all that he had made. I think because my father had tasted both wealth and poverty, that he wanted to make sure I never had to taste the latter."

She was silent for a while. I could tell it was painful for her to tell the rest of the story. I waited patiently.

"The Captain was somewhat of a hero in the Spanish-American War. He had a beautiful house, and wealth, he was respected, and unless the Great Lakes dried up, he had no chance of losing any of it. He had his eye on me, and my father decided that I would wed him."

"So your marriage was arranged?"

"Of course."

I had thought that arranged marriages predated this time considerably. But I was a stranger here in this time, and not being completely confident of my knowledge of the custom, decided I wouldn't ask her what she'd meant by her response.

"How long have you been married?"

"We were married in the summer of 1900. It was the second most unhappy day of my life."

I hesitated to ask, but I had to know.

"And what was the *most* unhappy day of your life, Kathleen?"

"Do you like *Longfellow*?"

"Of course, who doesn't?"

"He has a poem called *The Children's Hour*. Have you ever read it?"

"I love that poem."

"So do I. That was the way I always imagined my life would be. Little children, hanging all around my neck, all around my heart. It would have made up for the coldness of life with the Captain. I think that's why I finally went into teaching."

I didn't understand what she meant at first. But then it finally hit me, and I felt such sadness for her.

"You can't have children?" I paused, waiting for her to answer, but there was no need for her to answer. "Maybe it's him," I said, "Maybe . . ."

"Not if the rumors are true. He has a mistress in Chicago, and a mistress in Detroit. And children by both."

"My God, Kathleen, the man is an adulterer. Why don't you divorce him?"

"The Church would never allow it."

"To hell with the Church!"

She looked as though I'd just stabbed her in the heart.

"David, I cannot go against the things I truly believe."

"But Kathleen, this man has broken all the rules, even those of the Church."

"This man has the whole town, including all of the churches, in his dread. They would never dare go against him." She paused. "You asked me how I ended up with the Captain, and now you know. Could we talk about something more pleasant?"

"He beats you, doesn't he?"

"David, the whole town knows he does. Now can we *please* change the subject?"

"But then, what are you doing here with me today? You know he'll be furious if he finds out."

"I may be his wife, but I will not live in dread of him any longer. I will live my life. I will have my friends. And let the man beat me to death, if he will. But I will not live in a prison any longer."

What I wanted to do, was to go and find the man, and kill him at that very moment. Why not? I was the man that was supposed to kill him. I would eventually kill him anyway, according to history. Why not do it now, and get it over with? Would I use a gun? A knife? Maybe toothpicks, inserted one by one, over the period of a year, until he eventually died.

"David, what are you thinking about?" she asked, bringing me back to reality.

"Nothing pleasant. How could I waste these precious moments with you, thinking unpleasant thoughts?"

"Precisely," she answered with a smile.

Then she reached out and touched my hand. She touched me. My angel from 1905 touched me. Why? Kindness? Understanding? Was she saying that she knew I cared for her? Was she saying that she cared for *me*? She would *never* do anything against her beliefs. What was she saying?

I didn't know what to think, but I knew what I felt. That if I never spent another day in 1905, I would remember this moment, and bask in it, for the rest of my life.

We spent the rest of the afternoon exploring the shores of the island, and when we arrived back at the stables, the sun was setting. One of her servants took the horses, and Kathleen and I walked out to the bluff overlook. As I looked at the beauty of her profile, and her hair blowing in the wind, and the lighthouse in the background, I was awestruck.

"I wish I could capture on canvas, just what I see at this very moment," I said.

"You are an artist too?" she asked.

"No, and I've never wanted to be an artist, until this very moment. I'd like to be able to paint like Frank W. Benson. I'd paint *you*. And I'd paint every nook and cranny of this island."

"I've heard of him."

"Well, not many have. Mostly only other artists, now. And they think he paints too *pretty*. They're too caught up in their own sophisticated snobbery to appreciate the simple genius of his work. But someday they will. I just wish *everyone* could see what a great artist he was. Is."

She sat down on the bench, and I sat down beside her.

"David, I'm a school teacher. A teacher must be a patient observer, to know what to teach, and to know how to teach it. And I have made a very puzzling observation about you. The way you use language and verb tense . . . well, it is very puzzling. You talk about things in the future, as though they already are."

I understood immediately what she had observed.

"It has to do with where I'm from."

"Kansas? What do you mean?"

"Just do me a favor. If anyone ever invites you to ride on a boat called the Titanic, don't do it. Whatever you do, don't get on that boat."

As we sat there looking across the Straits, I thought about something she had said earlier. I know it was a silly question, motivated by insecurity, but I couldn't help but ask the question.

"And, Paul? Is he your friend?"

"I know what you're asking, and it's not what you're thinking. Paul and I have been friends since childhood, and we shall always be friends. Paul cares about my happiness."

"But he feels more for you."

"And he probably always will, David. But that is not how I feel. What about you? You must have a girl somewhere?"

"No. And God knows I've looked high and low. Not for the *perfect* woman. Just for the *right* one. Someone that would bring the best out in me, and I would do the same for her."

"Complementary opposites," she said, smiling.

"Yes. That's it. I've never had the words to describe it, but that's exactly it."

"It's the best kind of sameness there is."

"You make me feel so accepted. We've barely spent any time together, and yet, I feel like I could tell you anything. Share my deepest fears. My dearest dreams," I said.

"Good. I'm glad I make you feel comfortable."

"You make me feel a lot of things. Safe, for one. I've never met a woman that didn't make me feel like I was on trial. Or at least probation."

She laughed, and her laughter reminded me of the melody that I'd heard in my mind that first day I'd arrived on Mackinac Island.

"Kathleen, you are the kindest, most beautiful woman I have ever known. I've seen many beautiful women. But I've never known a woman that had . . . well . . . *supernatural beauty*, until I met you. There's a light inside you, more brilliant than that lighthouse."

I pointed across the Straits at the lighthouse. It was now dark, and its light was flashing across the Straits every seven or eight seconds.

She stood up and walked to the fence. She looked back at me.

"Maybe you *are*."

"Are what?" I asked, puzzled by her statement.

"On probation."

I walked over and stood beside her. She looked up at me and began to speak.

"Your letters meant so much to me. You can't possibly imagine. I had given up hope. You once said this place is like paradise. And I used to think of it that way. I used to feel safe. Protected. But when you feel trapped here, it's more like hell, than paradise."

"And you feel trapped here?"

"I've lived here all my life. I used to love this place. Some of the people that come here once or twice during the summer, and then say that they are from Mackinac Island, amuse me. It's like a medal that they pin on their lapels, to show others their class in society. Not all of them, but some. They don't know what this place is really about. I do. And I have always loved this place; until I married the Captain. And then I felt like my life was over. That this place was a prison, not paradise. Until your . . . your letters. See that room?" she said, pointing to the west end of the house.

"Up there?" I asked, pointing toward the turret.

She nodded. "That's where my dreams are. It's the only place I feel safe. I stay in that room when the Captain is away, which is most of the time. And I pretend that I'm in a castle fortress. I used to think, to hope, that someday, someone would come and rescue me."

"Dear God, I wish I could."

"You have, David. You *have*! I sit in that room and I read your letters, over and over. And I write to you. And I make copies of the letters I write to you before I send them. And I read those over and over, and think about how each word will make you feel. How I *hope* each word makes you feel. And I read each word of yours, and bask in their warmth. When I read our letters, I feel like I'm in paradise again. I feel like I'm home. How can I ever thank you?"

"Oh, Kathleen. Thank *me*? I need to thank *you*!" I gathered all my courage. I looked deeply into her eyes. "For the first time in my life, I . . ."

At that very moment there was a loud boom, and then a spray of colors across the sky above the Straits.

"It's Independence Day. I'd completely forgotten," she said.

"Me too," I answered.

"What were you going to say before the aerial display started?" she asked.

"I was going to say, that for the first time in my life . . ."

"There you are. I've been looking all over for you."

I was interrupted by the voice behind me. I turned to see John.

"Hi, Mrs. Sallee," John said.

"Hello, John," she said politely. But she was visibly upset at the interruption. "I need to go in now, Mr. Lovit. I shall see you at rehearsal on Saturday evening."

I started walking backwards down the hill, watching her as she walked up her stairs to stand on her porch to watch the fireworks. Only, she wasn't watching the fireworks. She was watching me. And I was watching her. And I wondered if I'd ever get another chance to tell her that I loved her.

## NINE
# Kathleen's Song

As we made our way down the hill, I tried to get John to tell me what was so urgent. He told me that Rand wanted to tell me himself, and when we finally got to the newspaper office, I found out why.

"Matty Johnson talked the opera house owners out of letting you do the play there. It doesn't surprise me. But I just didn't think it would come so soon," Rand said.

"Unbelievable. Doesn't that woman have a life?"

"No," Rand replied, as if I'd asked a really stupid question. And I guess I had.

"How did she do it?"

"She has her ways. She acts so innocuous, that's my big word for the day, but she collects dirt on people. But most likely, knowing Matty, she just talked them to death. That's pretty much how she gets everything she wants. Talks, and talks, and talks, and talks, until they just say *yes*, to get her to go away."

"I just can't believe it," I said.

"What did you expect, Lovit? The woman is over forty, has no husband, and the only thing she can even claim as an accomplishment in her life, is a bit-part in a play that was performed here twenty years ago. You peepeed on her golden calf."

"No one else cared. Everyone thought it was a great idea. Why should everyone else suffer just because she's so damned selfish?"

"You actually think a woman like that cares for anybody besides herself? Sure, you got everyone excited about this thing. Like they say: *A man awake with dawn in his eyes, multiplies.* But as *I* always say: *You can put out a campfire by peeing on it*, and that's just what she did."

"Damn it, damn it, damn it."

I felt so frustrated. So many people wanted this thing to happen, and they would be so disappointed. Especially Kathleen. She had such expectations. She was just beginning to feel like her life had hope again. How could I tell her?

\* \* \*

I spent the next three days avoiding the cast and crew. I felt horrible. I just couldn't face Kathleen, or Paul, or any of the others.

I knew I would have to break the news to everyone at rehearsal on Saturday. But I didn't have the nerve to face them as a group. So on Friday night, I decided I would make the rounds and let each person know one by one, saving Kathleen for last.

When I got to Paul's house, Paul's mother told me that he and the others were at the schoolhouse rehearsing. Now I felt even worse. They were rehearsing on their own. I would have to tell them all at once.

As I walked up to the schoolhouse, I could hear them rehearsing inside. I sat outside and listened for nearly an hour before I got up the nerve to go in. And listening to them made me feel even worse, because they were actually getting quite good.

As soon as I heard a break in the music, I walked in the front door. Everyone was smiling at me.

"Look, I have something I have to tell everyone," I said.

Paul spoke up. "What, that the play is canceled?"

"You know?" I looked at Kathleen, and she was still smiling.

"We've known since Wednesday afternoon. And we've been rehearsing every night, right here," Paul said.

"But we can't use the opera house, and there's not enough room here for an audience," I answered.

"It doesn't matter, David . . . ah, Mr. Lovit," Kathleen said. "There will always be people around like Matty. They aren't the problem. It's those of us who just lie down and give up. If we just quit, we are guaranteed failure. So doesn't it make more sense to keep acting as though it is going to happen? At least, this way, it has a chance. It's going to happen, David, It's going to happen."

"With people like you around, it sure will," I said to them all.

I felt very proud to be in the company of those people. I didn't know exactly who had rallied everyone on, but I suspected Kathleen and Paul must have had a big part in it.

The group rehearsed every night for the next three weeks. I was amazed at how polished they became. They could have performed on Broadway.

\* \* \*

Ever since I'd come across on the ferry that day, I'd had a melody in my mind. When I met Kathleen, the melody began to take on meaning, and began to become a song. The emotions it evoked were the same emotions that Kathleen evoked in my heart. Feelings of belonging, and of having come *home*. Feelings that I was where I was *meant* to be. Here on Mackinac Island. Here in 1905. Here with my Kathleen. I never wanted to leave her, or this island.

When no one was around, I would work on the song on the piano. I was writing it for *her*. I wanted to give it to her as a gift. A gift to let her know how I felt about her. To help her understand how she made me feel inside. To understand how much she meant to me, and to my life. To tell her how much I loved her.

It was around the middle of July that I had almost completely forgotten that I was from 1975. 1975 didn't make sense to me anymore. It was like a cartoon. More like a nightmare. Pseudo romance on the dance floor at the discos. Animalistic passions with no regard for life as a whole, or for other people's lives. It sickened me. And I didn't care if I ever went back there. Every time the thought of being from 1975 entered my mind, I would replace the thought with thoughts of Kathleen. I would sing her song in my mind, and become immersed in the emotions it evoked, and soon I would forget all about the future — at least the future that I had come from.

On Saturday night, July 29th, everyone seemed really worn out. I asked everyone to go home early. We'd rehearse the next Friday, August 4th, and have a dress rehearsal on the 5th, and that would be it until opening night on the 8th. They really had the material down, and I felt with any more rehearsing, their performances would become stagnant.

Everyone left except for Paul and Kathleen. It seemed like this was the perfect time to play the song I'd written for Kathleen. I asked her if she could stay for a few minutes, and then I walked Paul to the door as we talked about some miscellaneous details of the play.

We got outside the front door of the school, and he became very serious. He looked me in the eyes.

"If you ever hurt her, God help you," he said to me. And then he walked away.

I walked back into the schoolroom, and Kathleen was standing beside the piano. I knew it was time to play the song that I had written for her.

"I have a gift for you. I've written a song for you."

She smiled, but she didn't say a word.

I sat down at the piano. I didn't need sheet music. Every note was etched in my heart.

As I began to play the song, it was as though a symphony orchestra was playing along. And when I looked up from the keyboard into Kathleen's eyes, I could tell she heard it too. The sound was physical, tangible, like we could touch it, handle it. We both had entered a world neither of us had been in before, together. And it felt like home.

The song ended. And I again looked up from the keyboard into Kathleen's tear-filled eyes.

"Did you . . . ?"

"Yes, David, I could hear it all," she said, without even letting me finish. "Every single instrument."

"Did you like it?"

"You silly man," she said. And then she walked around beside me and put her hand on my shoulder. "How could you ask such a question?"

I could tell she had more to say, but was overcome with emotion, and couldn't speak. She was silent for quite a while, trying to find the right words to express her emotions.

"Some people talk and talk, and never say anything comprehensible. Your song . . . I mean, *my* song, had no lyrics. But I understood every single word."

There was no need to say more. I knew she did understand, because every word and note of the song had said, *I love you.*

Slowly, I rose from the piano bench and turned to face her. At that moment, the whole universe disappeared. Every physical item in the room — the piano, the stage, *everything* — disappeared. Only the two of us were left.

When I was a child, I had some large, very powerful magnets that I would play with. I'd arrange them so that their like-poles were facing, and I'd try with all my might to force them together. But I couldn't get them together. Eventually, the strong repelling forces would cause one of the magnets to flip over to its opposite pole, and then I couldn't get the magnets apart. That's how it felt at that moment. That no matter how much our *common sense* or *moral sense* pushed us away from each other, that in our hearts, we were being irresistibly drawn to each other.

I knew that I was the weak one. I had always felt that Kathleen was the strong one. And then, unexpectedly, Kathleen stepped toward me, closed her eyes, and moved her lips toward mine. Nothing in the universe could have stopped this from happening. This was meant to be. My heart raced. I move toward her and . . .

Where I got the strength from, I have no idea. I had dreamed of kissing this angel from the first moment I saw her picture at Murphy's. Maybe it was from remembering Murphy's. Remembering I wasn't supposed to be here. That I was from a different time altogether. Wherever the strength came from — or the stupidity, as you will — just before my lips touched hers, I moved my lips to her forehead, and kissed her gently.

I took a step back. She looked up at me. There was a light in her eyes. A look of admiration.

"Thank you, my friend," she said.

She turned and ran quickly toward the door. I was in such a daze, that she was at the door before I realized she wasn't standing in front of me anymore.

She stopped at the door and looked back at me. "That was the nicest birthday gift I've ever received."

"It's your birthday? I didn't know."

"That makes it even more special," she said.

She blew me a kiss, and ran out the door. I could hear her singing the melody of the song, as she ran down the sidewalk.

For most of my life, I'd never been happy with who I was — wished that I were someone else. Yet, at that moment, I wouldn't have traded places with any man in the world.

I was in love with Kathleen, and I knew that Kathleen was in love with me.

## TEN

# A Performance to Remember

It was Monday, August 7th, the night before the play, and I was sitting in the lobby of the Murphy Hotel, feeling somewhat depressed. In spite of the optimism of the cast and crew, we still hadn't found a place to present the play.

I was more disappointed for them than for myself. I knew how much the production meant to them, and how much they wanted to share it with others. But at the same time, I knew that they had given it their all, and that they felt successful about their involvement. They were in it for the right reasons.

"I have a message for a Mr. Lovit," I heard a voice behind me say.

I turned to see a young man in a Grand Hotel uniform. I took the message from him, opened it, and read: *Dear Mr. Lovit: Please meet me at seven o'clock this evening in my office at the Grand Hotel. Very important. Sincerely, Ez. Browning, Pres. Grand Hotel.*

It all seemed so clandestine, and I suddenly felt very uneasy. Had something happened to Kathleen?

Had someone found out about us? Were they going to banish me from the island, and from my Kathleen, forever?

As I made my way up the hill to the Grand Hotel, my mind rambled on and on. I walked into the hotel and toward the office, and my palms were sweating. When I got to the office door, it was opened slightly, and inside, I could see Kathleen, seated. Now I was *sure* I was in trouble.

Before I even had a chance to knock, I heard someone inside say, *Come in.* When I walked into the room, Kathleen was sitting next to Mary Browning. They were giggling in their usual fashion. Kathleen looked up at me, and she was smiling such a joyful smile.

"David. Ezekiel has such wonderful news," she said excitedly.

Ezekiel was visibly taken back by Kathleen's use of first names.

"Have a seat, Mr. Lovit," Ezekiel said, pointing to a chair on the opposite side of his desk from the ladies.

I sat down, and was somewhat relieved by the smiles in the room. But I couldn't imagine what in the world this *wonderful news* could be.

"I would like to help you with your play," Ezekiel said.

I about fell out of my chair.

"But, how? I don't understand."

"We've had one too many complaints about Miss Johnson. I, for one, am fed up with her meddling in everyone else's affairs. She may manipulate everyone else in her little web, but I won't stand for it. Why not present your play right here in our hotel theater?"

I was flabbergasted. This was beyond anything we had hoped for.

"I don't know what to say," I answered.

"I've heard some very good things about the production, and I think it will play very nicely here at our hotel. For the rest of the season, perhaps? And if it goes well, maybe a stint next season too. What do you think?" he asked me.

"I . . . again, I don't know what to say. I never even imagined this. This is wonderful. Thank you! Thank you!"

"Say nothing of it. I think it will please a lot of people." Then he stood and looked at his wife. "Well, dear, we should be going to dinner now. It was nice to see you again, Mr. . . . David. Kathleen."

He grinned as they walked out the door, and I thought of how incredibly nice it sounded, to hear someone speak our names together in the same sentence.

\* \* \*

By having the performances at the Grand, not only would the townspeople get to see the play, but we would have a built-in audience — the guests of the hotel. Summer visitors from all over the world.

Kathleen wrote a note to Paul, telling him the good news, and asking him to let the others know too. She gave the message to the hotel bellhop, and then we ran down the front steps of the Grand Hotel, arm in arm, laughing. We didn't care who saw us. Kathleen was so happy. And that was all that mattered to me.

As we walked up the hill toward Kathleen's house, I couldn't help but feel a little bit sorry for Matty Johnson.

"You know, Kathleen, I don't think Matty means harm. She's just a little misguided."

Kathleen looked at me like I'd just killed her beloved horse.

"Don't you *dare* try to justify her, David. While good people try so hard not to think ill of her, she climbs up over their backs. That's how she takes advantage of people. You know it, I know it, everybody knows it. That woman is a conniving, controlling witch."

Only she didn't say *witch*.

\* \* \*

As we walked up the hill toward her house, Kathleen took a deep breath.

"Can you smell them?" she asked. I could smell the fragrance of Elysium all around us. "That's how my life feels. Like it has fragrance again, David. I feel like this place is paradise."

It was so wonderful to see her happy. But at that very moment, I realized her happiness would be short lived.

"Kathleen, I'm sorry to bring this up, but, the play. We can only perform it for a week. Then the Captain will be back."

"Even if it were just for a week, I think I'd be happy for the rest of my life. But, David, it won't *be* just for a week. It shall be for the rest of my life. I'm leaving the Captain. I will not live in a prison any longer. I've waited all my life for you, and I will not let what we have slip away."

We walked up the steps to her front door in silence. She held out her hand to me. I took her hand in mine. I didn't want to let go. Neither did she. Then I broke the silence.

"I probably should go."

"It's unseasonably cool this evening. I was wondering if you'd mind making a fire for me before you leave?" she asked.

Neither of us said a word as I prepared the fire. When I finished, she walked over to the fireplace, and looked down into the fire.

"David, I feel as if this is the last time we will ever be together. I feel it so strongly."

I didn't want to acknowledge it. But I felt it too.

"All the servants are gone," she said, still looking into the fireplace. When she finally did look up, I could see a fire burning in her eyes.

"I have to go," I said, and I turned and headed toward the door.

"David!" I heard her voice from behind me. I knew I couldn't look back. I pushed the screen door open.

"David. Please stay!" she practically shouted.

I stopped dead in my tracks. And then I heard her say softly, "Don't go. Please."

I turned and walked slowly toward her, the whole time wondering if this *would* be the last time we would ever be together? I pulled her to me, and kissed her tenderly, the way I had dreamed a thousand times of kissing her since I'd first seen her picture that day in Murphy's. Then she looked up into my eyes, and neither of us said a word. She took me by the hand, and led me up the stairs to her favorite room. The room she loved. The one where her dreams were. And now mine would be there too.

*       *       *

"Good morning, my love."

I awoke to the most beautiful sound and sight in the world — the melody of Kathleen's voice, and her sweet face hovering over me. An angel's face. Standing there in her white lace garment, the sunlight from the window illuminating her silhouette, she looked like an angel.

"How do you know I'm not an angel?" she asked, knowing my thoughts.

"You *are* an angel," I said. "You've made my life too heavenly to be earthly."

"Well . . ." She paused as she walked to the window, and pulled the shades, blocking out the morning light. I watch the silhouette of her white lace gown fall from her shoulders and hit the floor.

"Who are you, and what have you done with my Kathleen?"

"You'll see," she said as she walked toward me, her eyes dark and mysterious with passion.

\* \* \*

It was noontime when I went out the back way by the stables, and down the back of Grand Hill. It was the opening night of the play, and I felt like I needed a couple of days sleep to prepare for the evening. But I didn't have time to sleep. The performance started at seven, and I only had a few hours to pull everything together.

The performers began arriving at the theater at six. By six-thirty, everyone had arrived but Kathleen and Paul. I put on Paul's British soldier costume, and was prepared to stumble through his part, if I had to.

"Has anyone seen Kathleen? The performance starts in thirty minutes. Someone get her understudy ready to go on."

"Paul isn't here either," someone said.

"I know that. Why in the hell do you think I'm in this costume?" I replied, wondering why I *was* in his costume, realizing that I didn't even know his lines.

At that moment, Paul ran in the back door.

"David. Captain Sallee is back," he said, trying to catch his breath.

"What? He's not supposed to be back for another week," I said in a panic.

"Matty Johnson sent him a letter telling him about Kathleen's involvement with the play — and with you."

"Paul, you've got to handle things here. I've got to go to her."

"Go, man. I'll handle it."

"Your costume?"

"There's another one. Go!" he commanded. "And Lovit, don't let that bastard hurt our girl anymore."

"I won't, I promise," I shouted back, and ran out the door.

It was only a short distance from the Grand to Kathleen's house. Just a minute or two, running. But it felt like it took *hours* to get there. When I reached the house, I could hear the Captain shouting from inside.

"You harlot. This will never happen again."

Then I heard Kathleen scream. I reached the screen door, and I could see Kathleen lying on the stairs, the Captain standing over her. I knew he had hit her. But then I saw what he had meant by his words, *this will never happen again.*

He had a gun in his hand. He had it pointed directly at her head. He pulled back the hammer. I couldn't let this happen.

"You son of a bitch. Only cowards bully women," I yelled at him, trying to get his attention off Kathleen.

It worked. Without missing a beat, he turned and pointed the gun directly at me. I could tell by the look in his eyes that he intended to use it, with no introductory statement.

I'd watched enough movies to know that the hero always gets out of these situations. And to be quite honest, I pictured myself as the hero in this situation. But this was not the movies. This was real life. This guy had a real gun. And I was going to be *real* dead. But in that same instant I thought; as soon as I was dead, this monster would kill Kathleen. And something clicked inside of me. This was not going to happen. There was no way I was going to let this happen. I'd just traveled seventy years from the future. I felt invincible, like I could walk on water. And why not? I already had.

I rushed toward him, and the gun went off. He had it pointed directly toward me. He was only a few feet away. But I knew, I knew it wouldn't hurt me. It would have to go through me, around me, under me. I didn't care. No one was going to hurt my Kathleen.

But in that very moment, I felt as if someone had just hit me in my right arm with a baseball bat. "Oh, God, I'm not invincible," I thought. I'd been shot. I fell to the floor. "This can't be happening."

Maybe it was his attempt to be honorable, but he dropped the pistol to the floor, walked to the wall above the fireplace, and took his saber from its case.

"And now you devil from hell, you shall die first," he said in a quiet, almost dignified, tone.

He reached inside his coat pocket and took something out, then tossed it toward me. It made a thump sound as it landed flat on my chest. It was my wallet — my 1975 wallet.

I would have resisted, but I couldn't move. Funny, the things that go through your mind when you're going to die. I thought about a dream I had when I was a child. I was under the kitchen table with a cat. The cat began to scratch me. I could see my mother's legs from under the table, and I tried to yell to her for help. But when I opened my mouth, nothing would come out. I would keep trying, but nothing would come out. Then I would awake in a panic, feeling totally helpless.

That's how I felt. Helpless. I couldn't even move to defend myself. I looked up and saw him position the blade of his saber, to thrust it through my heart. But I couldn't move. I closed my eyes. Surely this is a dream. Time travel. Ha! Right. 1905. Of course it's a dream. TEMPORALIS FISSVRA. LXX. ~>~. I will wake up. I will wake up. I've *got* to wake up.

A shot rang out. I opened my eyes. The Captain's eyes were filled with the same disbelief that mine were filled with only seconds before. He dropped the sword. It fell to his side. And then he fell backwards to the ground. There Kathleen stood, with the gun in her hands.

"I couldn't let him kill you," she said crying, dropping the gun to the floor.

Though I hadn't been able to move moments before, I got up, and practically ran across the room. I had almost complete control of my faculties now. It was fear that had frozen me moments before, and I felt ashamed that I had let it. That I had put Kathleen in the position of doing what she had to do.

I picked up the pistol and began handling it, putting my fingerprints all over it. I couldn't remember what year fingerprinting came into common use, but I wasn't taking any chances. At the same time, Kathleen tore off a piece of her dress, and wrapped it around my wound.

"You're bleeding," she said.

"Kathleen, go and wash your hands with the strongest soap you can find. Now!" I shouted at her.

I followed her to the kitchen. "Kathleen, when they question you, tell them that I came here, and that the Captain and I got in a fight, and that he shot me in the arm, and put his pistol down to get his saber, and that I picked up the pistol and shot him in the back. Have you got that?"

"I can't tell them that. *I* killed him," she said in tears.

"My love, they will hang you. Have no question about it." I pulled her close to me. "And I couldn't live with that. You shot him to defend me. Please, please, promise me that you will say what I told you to say."

"Yes, David, I will." She paused. "But if they catch you, I will tell them the truth. Because I could not live if *you* were to be hanged."

"They won't catch me," I said, still holding her tightly.

"David, you have to leave. Now! Go somewhere no one can find you."

"Temporalis Fissura," I said quietly.

"Where?" she asked, puzzled by my words.

"Someplace where no one will ever find me."

"Then go, my love. Go!"

I pulled her even closer. Would I ever hold her again after this night? I would have to remember this moment for all time. How could I forget my Katie? Her face, her smile, the way the sunlight lit her beautiful skin. Her long dark hair and the way it formed a perfect picture frame for such loveliness. The smell of her skin, the sound of her voice.

"Don't ever forget me, David."

"I'll be back. Somehow."

I ran out the front door, and down the sidewalk to the road. As soon as my feet hit the road, I heard someone shout, "STOP!" I looked down the hill toward the Grand, and a crowd of people were coming toward me. They'd heard the shot.

I ran to the top of the bluff, around the corner, and then up the back way toward Skull Cave. I knew if I could get back to the portal, I'd be safe. They couldn't follow me. I would go through the portal, back to my own time, and they would never know where I came from, or where I went. But when I got to the cave, there were people there already, looking inside and around the cave. This was my only escape, and I knew I'd have to wait until they were gone.

I hid in the bushes until it was completely dark, and then made my break for the rocks.

What happened next was too bizarre. Why I did this, I don't know. Maybe it was shock, the intensity of the moment, or because I was light headed from the blood I'd lost. Or because I'd just taken another man's life. Or because I'd just been forced to leave behind the love of my life. But, whatever the reason, without thinking, I climbed up the rocks, to the front side of the portal. By the time I'd realized what I'd done, it was too late. I saw men coming up the hill carrying torches, and I could hear their voices down on the ground.

"We've already looked here," I heard one man say to another.

"Yeah, well look again. I'll look over there," the other responded.

I knew if I waited any longer, they'd be up the rocks and find me hiding inside the opening. I had no choice. I didn't know what the consequence would be, but I had no choice. I had to go through the portal — from the front!

The night was pitch black, but I could feel the portal was covered with a large stone. I moved the stone and went through the portal, and then let the stone fall back over the opening as I went.

Immediately, I felt the same frequency drop, as before. As if life were slowing down by an octave, and then an octave again. Except this time, it was much lower, and there was an audible tone that dropped in frequency. Life seemed like it was in ultra slow motion. And I wasn't becoming acclimatized as I had before. The sound of the wind through the trees, sounded like the low pitched churning of the engines of a freighter going through the Straits. And as I moved my hand in front of me, it moved in slow motion, and left colorful trails in the full moonlight.

There hadn't *been* a moon in 1905. And from the way the moon sat in the sky, I could tell the time was later than when I'd entered the portal; perhaps one, maybe two o'clock in the morning.

And what was even stranger than the time difference was, that the ground was covered with snow. I didn't know where I was, or what year I was in. But I knew I couldn't stay. But I couldn't go back to 1905. Not yet. They'd still be looking for me.

I went around the rocks and climbed into the cave, hoping I'd be safe there until morning. I decided that I'd stay in the cave, just until daylight, and then go back to 1905. I'd get Kathleen, and we'd go away together. Where? I didn't know. But I would know in the morning. I just needed some rest. Just needed to get some sleep. My head would be clear in the morning. In the morning. I just needed some . . .

# Paradise
*Lost*?

## ELEVEN

## Out of the Frying Pan

When I awoke the next morning, my head was throbbing, my body was trembling, and the bright sunlight reflecting off of the snow from outside of the cave, blinded my eyes. I had lain there for several minutes with my hands over my eyes, trying to become accustomed to the light. As my vision returned, I could see a white form next to me. Then it took the shape of a face, and then . . .

"GEEZ!" I shouted, as I jumped backward, hitting my head on the cave wall.

It was a human skull. I looked around slowly. The whole cave was filled with skulls. And bones. I'd been sleeping on human bones.

"Let me out of here!" I said as I crawled out of the cave as quickly as I could.

I stood outside the cave in the bright sunshine. There was no road, only a snow-covered trail. And the air actually smelled sweeter and fresher than in 1905. I didn't know the year, but I knew it wasn't 1905. It was before. It had to be.

I'd become somewhat more acclimatized to my temporal location by now. There were no vision trails, and the sound was almost normal. But there was still an unreal quality to the atmosphere. Like this time was so far past, that it was beginning to fade. Almost as though it didn't *fully* exist anymore. And I was beginning to feel that way too; as though my own existence was fading.

I knew I needed to get back to my own time. Go back through the portal to 1905, and then quickly around the rocks, and through to 1975. There I could sort out everything. Get some medical help. Come up with a plan to get back to Kathleen.

I walked around to the back of the rocks, and walked toward the opening, when suddenly, my feet were kicked out from under me. I fell to the side and landed in the snow on my wounded arm. The pain was excruciating.

"Halt, you bloody bastard."

I looked up past the muzzle of the rifle that was less than a foot from my face, into the bloodshot eyes of a man that looked like he would have enjoyed pulling the trigger. He was hideously ugly, with teeth that were yellow and rotten, and he spoke with a Cockney accent. I could see under his animal skin coat, that he had on a red military uniform.

"Over here, sir," he shouted toward the woods.

I heard footsteps, and within seconds, six or seven men, dressed almost identically to him, stood over me.

"We've got ourselves a spy. That's the worst uniform I've ever seen," he said to the others.

They all laughed.

"Good work, Private Jones. Let's get him back to the fort," one of the others said.

Private Jones grabbed my wounded arm and pulled me to my feet. I cried out in pain. As they marched me down the hill and into the gates of the fort, he kept jabbing the muzzle of his gun into my back. And all the time I kept thinking about an old muzzle loader that my uncle used to own. The thing, on more than one occasion, had gone off for no reason whatsoever. And every time Jones poked that thing in my back, I kept thinking that it would be my last moment alive.

When we got to the blockade, *Mr. Handsome* opened the cell door and took personal joy into throwing me to the hard wooden floor.

"You can die here for all I care," he said as he walked out, slamming the blockade door behind him.

I had never been so afraid in all my life. I had no idea what they intended to do to me. Would they question me? Yes. But would they beat me? Torture me? I had nothing to tell them that they would believe. Dear God, would they execute me? Hang me? They'd probably put me in front of a firing squad. I'd die, and I wouldn't even know what year it was.

I had been in the blockade for about an hour, when I heard footsteps on the wooden walk outside the blockade, and then voices. Keys rattling, and then the door opening. My stomach was aching, and for the first time, I realized I was burning with fever.

"Merci," a man in a long dark robe said to the soldier guarding the door.

The man in the robe stepped into the room, and the door was closed. I heard the soldier locking it behind him.

"Who are you?" I asked, trembling from the fever.

"I'm Father Mark, my son," he said as he walked across the room. He put his hand on my forehead.

"What are they going to do to me?"

"Right now, nothing. We have to get you well," he said.

"Get me well so they can execute me?"

"Who are you, my son?"

"David Andrews . . . Lovit. What year is it?" I asked, delirious.

"You need to rest," he said, putting a wool blanket over my body. "And you need to eat something."

Within moments the door was unlocked, and an un-uniformed man came in carrying a large cup with steam rising from it. He gave it to Father Mark, and then left.

Father Mark fed me the soup, and every time I'd try to ask another question, he'd bring another spoonful to my mouth.

"I should have stayed in nineteen . . . I should have stayed with her. I should have . . ."

"Calm down, and rest," he said. The tone of his voice was comforting.

\* \* \*

I was far too weak to carry on a coherent conversation for several weeks. I'm quite sure that I would have died, had it not been for the kindness of Father Mark. He visited me every day, and his timing always seemed to be perfect. It was always about the same time *Mr. Handsome* would show up to relieve the guard for a meal.

I had no doubt that Private Jones would have killed me, if he'd had the chance, and then simply say he'd done it because I'd tried to escape. I had no idea why he hated me so. But I'd learned that some people just hate. Or at least, hate for reasons that have nothing to do with those they display their hatred toward.

I wasn't making excuses for anyone. I'd had a pretty rough childhood. And I realized at a certain age that I could have blamed my father for every bad thing that ever happened in my life, or take responsibility for my life. I knew his leaving had affected me, but I'd made up my mind that I was going to get over it, and do the best I could to make its effect on my life minimal. And the situation I was in wasn't anyone's fault but my own. Maybe I could blame it on the Captain. Then again, he thought he had a good reason for hating me; I had freed one of his slaves.

I'd learned from the guards' conversations that the year was 1814, and that I'd arrived there on the 11th of November. I wondered what would have happened, and how it would have affected the future, had I died there. Would I even be born? If I died in 1814, would I be there in 1905 to save Kathleen from the Captain? Or would Kathleen even be in the position of needing saving, if it wasn't for me? Just thinking about it made me dizzy. And it made me sick to think that I might have made things worse for Kathleen by ever going to 1905 at all.

\* \* \*

It was December 3$^{rd}$, 1814, and I'd been in the blockade for close to three weeks. The sun was shining, and it was warm for a December day. I was feeling better, but I hid my improved condition from the guards. I knew that if I were to escape, I'd need the advantage of the soldiers thinking I was still sick and weak.

Around noon that same day, Father Mark came to visit me. He tried to make conversation, but I was very reserved. I wanted to interact as little as possible with this time, and the people in it. But he was very perceptive, and soon he began (what seemed to me at the time) an inquisition regarding my mood.

"What is troubling you, my son?"

"Nothing, I just don't know what they are going to do to me," I said, trying to skirt the real issue that was on my mind.

"But there is something deeper troubling you, and I sense that you are out of harmony with the truth."

"*Whose* truth?" I said defensively. I don't know why I said it. I guess it was just a knee-jerk reaction, a defense mechanism from my college days at Cornell, when people used to try and beat me over the head with their ideas and beliefs. Now that Father Mark had helped me get well physically, I was afraid that he was going to try to *heal my soul*, and the last thing on earth that I wanted to hear was a sermon.

"There is a science to truth, even as there is a truth to science," he said.

"What do you mean?"

"I mean, if we walk into a laboratory, and we perform the exact same experiment, under the exact same conditions, we *both* shall get the exact same results. The laws of physics are universal."

"But *truth* is a different animal, Father. Everyone has a different opinion."

"Maybe we are not as honest in our quest for truth, as we are in the laboratory."

"That's for sure," I agreed.

"I have three great pursuits in life, my son. Science, philosophy, and truth. And truth is my foremost pursuit, because all true science, and all true philosophy, will harmonize accordingly."

"That would be quite a feat, for anyone to harmonize those subjects," I said, laughing.

"But it is really quite simple. Each must stay within the limits of its own domain."

"Meaning?"

"Meaning, that there are things in this universe that science *cannot* explain. And when it tries to, it forsakes empirical evidence, and embraces speculation, and is therefore, no longer science. Likewise, when philosophy moves from the realm of pure reason, its reason is no longer pure, because there are realities, *spiritual* realities, that the mind cannot comprehend."

"And so?"

"And so, we must seek truth to understand what is true science, and what is true philosophy, for truth is the essence and cause of the universe."

"And what do *you* believe truth is, Father?"

"Love. This is the truth that I have found, and all true science, and all true love of wisdom, will harmonize with this truth — the truth of love. This is why you and I are here, my friend. This is why we draw breath."

"Yeah, well. I'm not so sure," I said, wondering how much longer I'd be drawing breath. Wondering about all that had happened. And wondering if I'd done more harm than good. I began to feel like it would have been better if I'd never drawn breath at all.

Somehow, he must have sensed my thoughts, because the next words out of his mouth went straight to my heart.

"I'm afraid that we have all done things in the name of love, that weren't love. In science, it is possible to err, drawing wrong hypotheses and conclusions from our experiments, because of an unconsidered factor. But we must go back into the laboratory, and *include* that factor, and then try again. And so we must do also in life."

On the 4th of July, when Kathleen and I were at Skull Cave, I'd almost told her where I was from. But other than that one time, I'd never even been *tempted* to tell another soul about my situation. I really didn't *want* to tell anybody where I was from. Because 1905 was my home. Or at least I wanted it to be.

But, I had totally botched that. And now, I felt like I had to talk to someone about my dilemma, or explode. And for some reason, I felt like I could talk to this man. But I knew I couldn't give him the specifics. Yet, so much of my problem *revolved* around the specifics; that I had *defied* the laws of science and physics, and gone someplace — some *time* — that I probably should have never gone to, to begin with.

If I tried to tell him I was from 1975, he would think I was crazy. If I spoke in generalities, I knew he would sense my guardedness; plus I knew some philosopher had said, *generalities are the refuge of weak minds*, and I sure in hell didn't want him to think I had a weak mind.

"This isn't like a confession, or anything, is it? Because I'm not even Catholic," I said.

"My allegiance is not to an institution. My allegiance is to one and one only. To the greatest force in the universe; the cause of the universe — love."

"Well, I'm not looking for absolution. And besides, I'm not even sure if I've done anything wrong."

"You think you have made a mistake, no?"

"I don't know. It's all pretty complicated."

"To err is human, and so we err. This is why we humans have such a hard time believing in an unerring truth. You may have had an experiment fail in the laboratory, but the laws of physics do not change to accommodate your failure. They remain the same. And thus, so does truth. And it is this truth that you must discover, and it is this truth from which you hide."

"I'm not so sure what the truth in my situation is," I answered. He had no idea what my situation was anyway, so even if I was *hiding from the truth*, how in the hell would he know?

"The truth is not hidden, my friend, but hidden *from*."

I was starting to feel like I was talking to a broken record.

"Guess it all depends on whose concept of truth you're talking about."

"And whose concept is the sky, the water, the planets, the universe?" he came back.

"The universe is whoever's concept you think it is. Everything is relative," the Cornell grad in me said, battling his concept of universal truth.

"Yes, but relative to what? Every chord has its root. Every melody has its tonis, ah, tonic as you would say. Every note has its fundamental vibration. There is a fundamental to all harmony, a constant vibration to which all other vibrations bear their relationship. This fundamental is the basis of harmony."

"So what is this fundamental *truth* I'm hiding from, Father?" I said, annoyed with his insistence.

"I have told you. The truth is love. Love is the fundamental of universal harmony. It is the tonis that all other notes must align with, in order to harmonize. And the love of the truth; that is the harmony, the alignment."

I'd become quite good at *winning* philosophical arguments from my days at Cornell. And I say *winning*, because, quite honestly, in my heart, I really *did* believe in the concept of *universal truth*. But it wasn't *cool*, or *in*, and I really wanted to be accepted by my peers. So, it didn't matter how logical the other person's argument was. The goal was to *win* the argument, at any cost, at any sacrifice of principle. And I'd collected a whole bag full of mind tricks to throw at anyone who backed me into a corner with an argument I couldn't rebut.

At that moment, I felt backed into a corner. And I'd learned if the *everything's relative* redirection didn't work, just start redefining words *to infinity*.

"And what is love?" I asked him.

He had been very patient, but was slowly becoming impatient with my defensive strategies.

"Your arguments, my friend, are written in text books, and institutional dogma. Mine are written in the stars, and have been from the foundation of the cosmos. You ask me what love is? Some are willing to give up truth for their lives or livelihood, while others are willing to give their livelihood or lives, for truth. You tell *me* which is an act of selfishness, and which is an act of love."

He paused. Then he smiled, and looked me in the eyes. "I cannot tell you what you must do in your situation. Only you can know, and only you can do it. But there is a way of love and harmony, and there is a way of discord and dissonance."

To me, music was both a language of science and love. And he had been using a nomenclature that I could totally relate to. A vocabulary that reached my heart. That of music.

"I do want to do the right thing. But, like I said, it's all gotten pretty complicated."

He thought for a moment about what I'd said, and then spoke. "In life, there are simple harmonies. And then there are more *complex* harmonies; overtones that have a more distant mathematical ratio to their fundamental. Remember your tonal center, and you may explore love's complexities. Lose it, and you drift further and further from harmony."

"We're not talking about a song that I can simply stop and start over, or simply change keys," I said.

"No. We are talking about life, my friend. We are talking about life."

I pondered his words for a while. Not just the content, but the form he had chosen, and his knowledge of music and its science.

"I can tell by your use of musical terminology and analogy, that we share a love of music," I said.

"Yes, and I can tell by your mannerisms, my friend, that we share a love of *time*."

I sat there for several moments before I realized what his statement meant. Then suddenly, it hit me. *He* was a time traveler too!

## TWELVE
# The Secret

I had a million questions I wanted to ask him, and things I wanted him to explain to me, like: *what year was he from? And why was it that, when I went back from 1975, I ended up in 1905 — 70 years earlier to the day? But when I went back from 1905, I ended up in 1814 — 90 years and some odd months earlier, and in the middle of winter? And how in the hell did the portal get there to begin with?* I had so many questions, I didn't know which one to ask first. And before I had a chance to ask anything, he spoke.

"You picked a fine time to arrive here. You are in the middle of a war. And, the Lord help you, why are you in that uniform?"

"It's a costume. I was in a play."

"And a bad costume, at that. Your circumstances are not smiling on you, my friend. They think you are a spy."

Of all the bum hands I'd ever been dealt, it seemed this was the worst set of circumstances possible. And just when I thought it couldn't get any worse, Father Mark had more *good news*.

"There's talk of negotiations, and that the war will be over before the new year. But they will probably try to get rid of you before the treaty is signed. They don't like spies. We must get you out of here. But I don't know how we are going to do it."

"I have so many questions for you," I said.

"About the time portal?"

"Yes."

"And you think I have the answers?"

"I hoped . . . well, you were here before me. You must know *something*."

"I am very careful to keep science, philosophy, and truth, in their respective domains. And I don't understand this from any aspect. I have a hypothesis. But that is all. Just a hypothesis."

"I'm listening."

"Did you happen to discover that you couldn't go forward from your time?" he asked me.

I had never walked to the back of the rocks in my own time. But when I took *Kathleen* to the back of the rocks, she couldn't see the opening. I realized that must have been true of my time also.

"It's a one-way opening, isn't it? I mean, it will allow one to go back from their own time, but not any further *forward* than their own time," I said.

"Precisely."

"And where, what time, are you from?"

"I've been trying to figure out where *you* are from. And I'm a little confused. But from observing you these past several weeks, my guess is, you are from close to my time. But you've had an extended visit, somewhere between 1896, and 1912."

"You can tell that?"

"Just a guess."

"Good guess. But you never did answer me. What year are you from?"

"I left in 1955."

"I'm from 1975."

"Well, I was close. Besides, it's all relative," he said with a grin. "Time and space, that is," he added.

"And what about the distance in years, as one goes through the front of the portal again?" I asked.

"It increases every time you loop through the portal. The span gets longer, but I have yet to find an algorithm to which the increase will conform."

"But why can't one go forward from their own time?"

"My theory — again, it's only a theory — is that . . ." He paused for quite a while, and then finally finished his sentence. "That there is no future."

"What do you mean, no future?"

"That *now* and *is* are one and the same. And that the past that we are in is only . . ."

"Only what?"

"That the present is like a comet, and the past is only its trail — its burning embers. We can't go forward from our time. No one can, because there *is* no forward. But we can go back, or maybe a better way to put it would be, we can slow ourselves down and view the fading image of what has already been."

"We're living in an echo? A ghost town?" I hated the thought. To think of Kathleen, for even a second, as anything but alive and vibrant, was detestable. "But that makes no sense," I said. "We are not just *viewing* the past. We are *participating* in it."

"Like I said, it's a theory. A very *untested* theory. I mean, how does one go about testing it?"

"And temporalis fissura?"

He paused for a moment, puzzled by what I'd just said. "Time fissure. That's a very fitting name."

"Didn't you name it that?" I asked.

He looked even more puzzled.

"The covering? Didn't you engrave those words on the stone over the portal?" I asked.

"I know of no stone. No engraving," he answered.

So strange. Were there others that had used this portal?

"And the portal. What is it? How did it get there?" I asked.

"I suppose it is some kind of link. How it got there? Again, I have a theory."

I listened intently.

"There is something special about this island. Some attraction, some association, with time and timelessness. I feel that *time* will always be connected with this island."

"I felt that. When I first arrived here on the island, I felt it. Like the whole island was resisting the movement of time," I said.

"Maybe it's like that hole you have in the elbow of your shirt," he said, pointing to my left sleeve. "It didn't happen all at once. But your elbow just kept rubbing and rubbing against it, until it wore through. Maybe in an attempt to preserve the island's timelessness, it has become a meeting place for those who long for simpler times; a hole in the elbow of the shirt of time, so to speak," he said laughing.

I offered my own hypothesis. "Maybe. But maybe it's like *this* hole," I said, pointing to the bloodstained hole in my right arm where I'd been shot.

As I looked at the bandages underneath my shirt, I panicked. I remembered that Kathleen had wrapped a piece of her dress around my wound, and I realized I didn't know what happened to it. Father Mark could tell I was upset.

"Yes, maybe something cataclysmic *tore* the hole. I don't think we'll ever know. In my opinion, the only thing strong enough to tear a hole in time, would be love," he said.

And with that, he sighed deeply, stood up, and walked to the door. I could see he didn't want to talk anymore. But I had to know.

"Why did you go back in time?" I asked him.

"I saw the world becoming more narcissistic, more selfish. More concerned with aesthetics, pleasure, and power. Love, true love, had been all but forgotten. My heart became sick. I thought, hoped, that maybe I could . . ."

I cut him off. "You were in love with someone. A romance."

"My son, there is a love that surpasses romantic love. It is called sacrificial love, and it is the most romantic love that I have ever known."

\* \* \*

He kept coming back to this theme of *love*, and now he was talking about *sacrificial* love. I wasn't sure I liked the sound of those words together in the same sentence.

"Sacrificial love. The kind of love that gives, instead of takes. It is true love," he said without my asking him for further definition.

His explanation of sacrificial love struck a chord, because Kathleen and I had written in our letters many times of this very thing: a love that gives instead of takes. A *pure* love.

"Have you ever been in love, Father? I mean romantically?"

"I *thought* I was. She was a beautiful, beautiful girl. I would have made a statue of her, if I could have. I worshiped her, and the ground she walked on. She was everything I had ever wanted. But I realized one day, that I was not everything that *she* wanted. And so, I ended it. It was only a matter of time before she would have ended it, anyway. But I still pined for her for years. Until one day I realized that everything she was, was what I'd made her in my own mind. And when I did, the pain went away."

"But it's not that way with Kathleen and me. We truly love each other."

"Ah!" He reached in his pocket, and took out the piece of dress that Kathleen had wrapped around my wound. "Which explains *this*." He handed it to me. "It is hers, no?"

"Yes," I said as I took it. I held it tightly in my hands.

"I did not mean to insinuate that your situation was like mine. But there is a bullet wound, and her cloth was wrapped around it. So I can see that all is not simple in paradise."

"And I'm afraid I may have made things worse."

"Only you can decide what is the best way to resolve your situation. But sometimes the correct resolution involves sacrifice. Doing something that you don't want to do at the time. You, my friend, have jumped from love's sweet warmth, into its fire, and it will prove the very depths of the trueness of your love. And you cannot run away from it."

"I don't want to run away from it. For the first time in my life, I care about something, someone, more than my own life. I want to be with her. To care for her. To make sure she is all right."

"Maybe you have already done for her what you were *meant* to do for her."

"But she is my destiny. My fate."

"Love is a decision, not an inescapable fate. To harmonize in its beauty, must be done one note at a time. One resolution at a time. Even a single note of true love, is like dropping a pebble in the waters of life. It will radiate outward until every edge of the pond has been touched by its beauty."

"But how do I know which is the right note?"

"I have heard it said, that there are no incorrect notes, only incorrect resolutions. And this seems to be your dilemma. Resolution. No?"

"Yes."

"You will know. Time will tell. *Love* will tell. You cannot resolve your whole life with one note. You must resolve each note of your life, one note at a time. And this, my friend, is how the symphony of your life must be played."

"But what will happen to . . . ?"

"You may not see the results immediately, but you will see them someday. And they will resonate in your heart, and in hers, for longer than you can possibly imagine."

"You mean forever?"

"That which is in harmony with love, will last forever."

"You say that an act of true love is like dropping a pebble in a pond. But what about acts of selfishness, and evil? The kindest person I have ever known, was beaten and battered by one of the cruelest, most arrogant people I have ever known. It seems to me that these acts are like someone throwing a *boulder* in the pond."

"Unfortunately, those who choose not to live in harmony with love, also affect those who do. But the effect of good will outweigh the consequence of evil. And the evil that this man has done will come back to him someday. Even as the good you have done, it will come back to *you* someday."

"This man's evil has already come back to him. He's dead."

"Then this is justice. What he gave out, returned to him."

"And Private Jones. Will all that he is giving out come back to *him* someday?"

"It is inescapable."

"Well, I sure hope it comes back to him soon, before he gets a chance to kill me. And as far as good triumphing over evil; just for your information, things aren't getting any better in the future. You know? The 1975 future," I said.

"That is sad. I came back here hoping that what I did here would affect the future. That is very sad indeed."

"Why don't you go to 1975? With all you've learned here, you could probably help change things," I said.

"Why don't *you* go back? I mean forward?" he asked me. "You don't go back, because you found something, someone, worth staying for. Right?"

"And you found someone?"

"I found *many* someones. And besides, do you really think there is anything worth going forward for?"

"But there have been *tremendous* advances in science, technology, and medicine, since 1955. You'd be amazed," I said.

"Your society, the society that I left, creates a need, then creates a solution to the need it has created. And then pats its self-righteous self on the back for doing it. For being so resourceful, intelligent and benevolent."

"You're right. But maybe they can be taught?"

"For every lesson they learn, they forget ten other lessons. They retain nothing." He pointed toward the front of the blockade. "In my time, your time, there is a statue that sits in the park, at the base of this fort. No one will remember why it's there, or what they wanted to remind themselves of by putting it there. I've watched people from every era struggle with their own identity. Watched them trying to figure out who they are. Limited by their own selfishness, they worship and enshrine others. Worship and enshrine institutions, and then recite the same boring chants that others inscribe for them. They've learned nothing."

I agreed with him, and I had left 1975 to begin with, because of these modern dilemmas. But I felt like I should play the devil's advocate, for argument's sake. "How can you downplay technology? Or the advancements that have been made socially?" I asked him.

"Advancements? Your society is built on economic and aesthetic rationalizations. You don't educate men and women to be good thinkers, but to be good rationalizers, good talkers, good persuaders, and good selfish money makers. Why should I return to that? Science and philosophy have just become economic and political tools, and that is why science is no longer science, and philosophy is no longer a love of wisdom."

"What you're doing here. It must be helping. Certainly you — we — must be making a difference," I said.

"I don't know. I hope so. I don't think we will ever understand the past. They do things differently here. And the only way to even come close to visiting the past accurately, is the way we have done it. And even that is tainted, because we still bring with us our current-day perspectives. The longer I'm here, the more I understand why they do as they do. We may have done some good. But there is so much imbalance in the future, I don't know if anything we are doing here in the past is helping *correct* it. Maybe our being here has contributed to the problems in our times," he said.

"What you're saying sounds pretty fatalistic to me. I can't accept that. I *don't* accept it. I agree that, there are far more things that I would change in the future, than here. But I think, hope to God, that some of the changes are real."

"Whenever and wherever love is the impetus, the changes are real and lasting. Wherever force, resentment, money and power are the motives, injustices have simply shifted. And injustice is *never* justified, for it is outside the harmony of love."

"So have we made a difference?"

"I hope so, my friend. I hope so."

"And where does *time* fit into all of this?" I asked him.

"As someone once said, or *will* say, *Time is the stuff that life is made of.* So don't waste it, my friend. For it is the tempo in which the notes of love must be played."

"Yeah, well if I don't get out of here, I'm afraid my little tune is over."

"You will have at least one chance to escape. There may be *only* one. But there will be at *least* one."

## THIRTEEN
# A Change in Tempo

It had been nearly a month since I'd arrived in 1814. I had to find a way out of the blockade. Find a way to get back to Kathleen.

In one corner of the ceiling was a weakness I felt I could exploit. Some of the roofing was coming loose, and I could see it lift every time the wind blew. Each day when the guard thought I was resting, he would walk out into the yard to chat with his buddies. And when he did, I would climb onto a beam and quietly loosen the roofing even more. But not so much that it would blow away in the wind.

I studied the guards, their habits, and the signs of their changing. The canteen wall adjoined the blockade wall, and I began to recognize their voices, and associate their voices with their names. And every night, shortly after the changing of the guard, I would hear the voice of the guard that was supposed to be watching the blockade. Only, not from outside my cell, but from inside the canteen.

It would only be for a few minutes, but without fail, every night, he would be in the canteen.

He'd guzzle down a quick ale, and then take his post back outside the blockade. I realized this would be my window of opportunity.

*   *   *

I'd planned to escape that very evening. But in the afternoon, Father Mark didn't show for his usual visit. As I was waiting for him to show, I heard the keys jingling outside the cell. The door opened, and in walked Private Jones. I tried to act like I was sleeping, but it didn't do any good. He came across the room and grabbed my wounded arm, and pulled me to my feet. I knew that if I cried out for help, I'd be dead. Shot, "trying to escape."

I didn't say a word. He pulled me to one corner of the room where there was a small padlocked door in the floor. He threw me to the floor next to it. He opened it, and then kept kicking me in the side, until I fell down into the hole.

"You ain't as sick as you're tryin' to make everybody think," he said. Then he slammed the trap door shut. I heard the padlock click, and then his footsteps as he crossed the blockade floor. I could hear the faint sound of the blockade door as it shut.

Even though it was day, I couldn't see anything. Slowly my eyes became accustomed to the light, and I could see that the area I was in was about 6 feet by 6 feet, and maybe 4 feet high. It had a dirt floor, and its walls were made of large stones, stacked on top of one another. The ceiling was the floor of the canteen, and I could hear people walking overhead.

I wasn't sure, but I thought that Jones might have broken one or two of my ribs. But I was thankful that though he'd grabbed my wounded arm, he hadn't opened the wound back up.

\*   \*   \*

Several days went by, but Father Mark never came to visit. I didn't know if he was dead, or what they had done to him. But I knew *I* wasn't going to be alive much longer. Because, that morning I heard them talking in the canteen about a subject I didn't want to hear. My execution. I was to be executed in two days. Without a trial.

\*   \*   \*

For the next day and a half, I was totally despondent. I had traveled through time. I had loved. I had lost. I just wanted it all to be over. It was so cold, and damp, and dark. I felt as if I were already *in* a grave. And I probably would have given up. But I began to think about what Father Mark had said about sacrificial love. If I was going to die, I didn't want to die like this. For no purpose. I wanted my life, or at least my death, to count for something.

The more I thought about it, the more I began to question myself for the position I'd put Kathleen in. Yes, I'd saved her life, and saved her from the abuse of the Captain. But now, her heart was completely entwined with mine, as mine was with hers. And I was a fugitive. What kind of a life could I give her in her time? And I couldn't take her back to my time, because for her, there was no future. I couldn't bring her back here, because here too, I was a criminal. What if I took her back further? Those times would have been too hard. Too primitive. Too isolated.

I began to feel that my love for Kathleen was selfish. That I had helped her in one way, only to hurt her in another. If I truly loved Kathleen, I knew I would have to do the hardest thing that I had ever done in my life — to let her have her life back. If what Father Mark had said was true, about there not being any incorrect notes, only incorrect resolutions, then I knew that I had a chance to resolve this, correctly. In harmony with love.

When I was younger, I had a poster on my wall. The one about, *If you love something let it go, if it comes back to you it's yours, if not, it was never yours to begin with,* ad infinitum, ad nauseaum. I hated that poster. My roommate and I had crossed out the words: *if not, it was never yours to begin with,* and substituted the words: *if not, shoot the bitch for cheating,* or some other ridiculous phrase of the week.

Now, I hated the poster more than ever. Because I *did* love something. Some *one.* And I realized, that in this particular situation, the words of the poster applied. And the worst part was, I knew that we would never be together again. Ever!

I had promised her that I'd be back. But I knew that if I really cared about her life, that I couldn't keep my word. But I couldn't let her think that I'd just abandoned her. I had to find a way to let her know. I had to get out of this hole, get back to 1905, and somehow, let her know. Let her know that I hadn't forgotten her. Let her know why I wouldn't be coming back. I needed to resolve this note, this progression, this cadence, in both of our lives, in a way that would be right. I couldn't just give up and die.

\*   \*   \*

It was close to midnight, and I was to be executed in the morning. I had about eight hours to escape, and I kept thinking about something Father Mark had said. He said that I'd have at least one chance to escape. And I felt like I'd already blown my one chance. But then something happened that gave me hope.

There had been a lot of snow in November. But the December days had been quite warm. And the runoff from the melting snow had been pouring into the hole for the last several days. I hadn't realized it, but the runoff had started to erode the foundation underneath the canteen.

I loosened a medium sized stone from the floor, and started digging away the dirt. It wasn't much, but it was enough so I could wedge my body between the floor joists, and the ground, and inch my way toward the outside wall of the canteen. I had to dig quietly, so I wouldn't alert the soldiers in the canteen above. But I kept digging, and finally loosened a large stone from the foundation. I pulled the stone out, and the opening was just big enough that I could crawl through.

The guard would be changing shortly, and I waited there until I heard the voice of my guard, going into the canteen for his nightly *quick one.*

I could still hear the guard as I inched my way through the foundation, and then, nothing. I didn't know if he had left the canteen, or what. I made my way quietly around the blockade and through the yard, toward a low spot in the wall at the back of the fort.

"Hold it right there," I heard a voice say.

It was him. The guard. He had his gun pointed at me, and was bringing his whistle to his mouth to blow it. But at that very moment, I heard a thud, and saw the man's eyes roll up into his head. He went limp, and collapsed to the ground. He was out cold. Lying next to his head was a large stone. And out from behind the building came Father Mark.

"Where have you been? Are you all right?" I asked him.

"It seems I have fallen out of favor with the British. I'm sure this will not help the matter," he said, as he put his hands together in a yoke, to help me over the wall.

"What are you going to do?" I asked as he began to hoist me up the wall.

"I'm going through the portal," he said grunting, as he gave me a foot up to the top of the wall.

I held out my hand, and helped him up on the wall. We both jumped down to the ground on the other side, and headed east up the road.

"To 1975?" I asked him.

"No. Further into the past," he answered. "I've been there before."

"How far back have you been?" I asked, surprised by this revelation.

"Far enough to know that history resembles legend, more than so-called science. I've been back until the image was almost ghostly, almost completely nonexistent; just shadows and blurs."

"And why are you going back now?" I asked.

"I have to finish something I started there," he said, smiling.

We came to a fork in the road, and he stopped.

"I have to get some of my books first. But you must go now. Go, now! And make sure you go through the back of the portal this time," he said with a grin.

"And *you* make sure you go through the front," I said, countering. "Thank you. For everything, Father."

"Please call me Jacques."

I turned to go up the hill toward Skull Cave, when I suddenly realized who this time traveler was. I turned around.

"You're Marquette! They'll erect a statue of you here on this island someday."

"Not if you talk any louder, they won't. Besides, I've seen it. Horrible likeness," he said as he disappeared into the darkness.

\* \* \*

I ran up the hill to Skull Cave. I didn't see a soul as I made my way there, and didn't hear anyone pursuing. My heart raced when I realized that finally I would be able to see my Kathleen, if only for a few precious moments.

I was within five feet of the opening, when out of the woods stepped Private Jones. He had his gun raised and pointed toward me.

"Take another step and I'll kill you."

I froze.

"Actually, I think I'll kill you anyway. But I want you to watch it happening. I want you to look me in the eyes, and hear the crack of the rifle, before it rips your bloody head off."

I had to think fast.

"Fine, Jones. You win. You've got me. I've had enough."

"Stand against that wall over there. We'll have our own little execution by firing squad, you and me. Only you don't get no blindfold."

I walked to the opening of the portal and stood there. Even though I could see the opening in the rocks, I knew *he* couldn't — unless of course, he was *also* a time traveler. Which in that case, I was pretty well out of luck anyway.

I turned and faced him.

"Goodbye," he said, with a malicious grin, as he cocked the hammer of his gun.

"Goodbye, you miserable son of a bitch," I said, as I turned and jumped headfirst into the portal.

I heard the sound of the shot, and then the ricochet. I turned around, and looked back through the portal. Jones was still standing. He had a look of shock on his face, and blood was dripping from the one inch hole in his head. He fell to the ground, dead from his own bullet.

I thought about what Father Mark had said about this man. That his evil would all come back to him someday. If ever I felt there was any justice in the world, it was at that moment.

## FOURTEEN
# Such Sweet Sorrow?

When I came out of the portal into 1905, it was a warm night, with a full moon. Judging by the position of the moon, it was probably around ten o'clock. I had been in 1814 for close to a month, and I knew that the portal would allow for the same relative passing of time, even as it had before. So as best as I could tell, the date was somewhere around the 6th or 7th of September.

I went down the trail toward the back of the Grand Hotel. Whenever I heard someone, I hid in the brush. If anyone saw me, they would definitely recognize me, even in my costume. *Especially* in my costume. I had to get to the dressing rooms at the theater, and get some other clothes on. Get a disguise. Then I would go to Kathleen's house, and try to explain to her why I had to leave. Try to say goodbye to the only woman that I had ever loved.

I went into the theater through the back way, and then into one of the dressing rooms. I glanced at the mirror, and was startled at first, thinking that someone else was there. Then I realized it was my own reflection — with a full month's growth of hair on my face.

I found some scissors, and trimmed my beard and mustache. On one of the dressing tables was a water basin, with a small amount of water in it. I used the little bit of water to clean myself up as best as I could.

Hanging on the costume rack was a tux, and on top of the rack was a hat. I took off my costume and stuffed it in one of the dressing table drawers. Then I put on the tux and hat, and some prop-glasses, and headed out the back of the hotel, up past Kathleen's stables, and around the corner to the bluff overlook.

When I reached the bluff overlook, I stood in the cover of the shadows, and watched as the full moon danced on the water, the steady flash of the lighthouse keeping time. It reminded me that Kathleen and I had never danced together. And for a moment, I pictured us in the Grand Hotel ballroom, dancing together. Smiling. Happy.

I was brought back to reality when I heard the front screen door of the wedding cake house shut. I'm not sure if I was afraid to look back because of what I might see, or because of what I might *not* see. If I looked back and she wasn't there, I was sure I would die at that very moment. If I looked back and she *was* standing on the porch, I knew that I wouldn't be able to tell her any of the things I'd planned. I'd break.

But I finally did look. And when I did, there was Kathleen, standing on the porch. She was crying. And there on the porch with her was Paul. He was holding her, comforting her. And suddenly I knew. That it was the best thing. It was the right thing.

At that moment I knew what I needed to say to her, and I knew exactly *how* I needed to say it.

I walked back up past the stables, and then down Grand Hill, and around to the front of the hotel. I walked to the front desk and asked for some stationery. What I needed to say to her, needed to be said in a letter. It was the way we had come to know each other's hearts to begin with. It was the way we understood each other best. And it was the way I needed to say goodbye.

*Thursday, Sept 7<sup>th</sup>, 1905*

*My Dearest Kathleen,*

*Writing to you has always been so very easy. But this letter is so very difficult. The most difficult letter I've ever had to write in my life, and the shorter it is, the better it probably is, for both of us.*

*I love you more than my own life, my dearest, and even though what I'm about to tell you will hurt us both, it's what I must do, <u>because</u> I love you. I must say goodbye. You may not understand why now, but I believe that someday you will know that my motive was love. True love. The love that we wrote about in our letters — the kind of love that gives instead of takes.*

*There are no words to thank you, my angel, for what you have done for my life. Please know that I love you more than life itself, and please, please know that I will never ever forget you.*

*Yours, of course.*
*David*

"Would you please see that Kathleen Sallee gets this?" I said, handing it to the desk clerk.

I walked out of the Grand Hotel, and down the hill to the Gazette. There was no reason to hide anymore. The desk clerk had seen me many times, and he hadn't recognized me in the tux, with my beard and the prop-glasses, so how would anyone else?

I walked into the Gazette. I just wanted to see the place one more time before I left 1905 forever.

"Hold it right there," I heard a voice say. I saw the figure of someone in the dark, and the silhouette of a gun. Then the man stepped forward. "Is that you, Lovit?"

"Yes," I answered, recognizing Rand's voice.

"Jesus, you scared the crap out of us," he said.

John stepped out of the shadows too.

"Are you going to turn me in?" I asked Rand.

"Turn you in? Are you kidding? You're a hero. The bastard *deserved* to die."

He turned to John, and hit him over the head with a rolled up newspaper.

"And what in the hell are you looking at, you little bastard? He *did* deserve to die."

"I know," John said to Rand. Then John looked at me with a smile and said, "You've given us a lot to write about. We even printed on Saturday and Sunday."

"Go on, get out of here, before we have to print a headline that reads: *Murderer of Miserable Lakes Captain Apprehended*," Rand said. "My boat is down on the dock. Take her anywhere you want."

"That's ok, Rand. I've got my own way out.
But I will take a stick of your fishing dynamite, if you
don't mind."

He looked bewildered at my request, but
handed me the dynamite.

"Oh, great! *Murderer of Miserable Lakes Captain
Apprehended while Fishing with Dynamite*," he said.

"I've gotta go. Thanks for everything, Rand.
You too, John. I'm going to miss you both."

"Oh, go on. Get out of here. No reason to get
all lugubrious. And Kathleen? Are you gonna take her
with you, man?" Rand asked.

"She'll be all right, Rand. She'll be all right."

\*   \*   \*

When I was a child, I could never figure out
why in the world Dorothy wanted to leave Oz to go
back to Kansas. I remembered the day I came to
Mackinac Island on the ferry, and that I felt like I was
coming home. But it wasn't Mackinac Island of 1975
that was my home. It was Mackinac Island of 1905.
And Kathleen. She was my home. And now I was
leaving. Leaving my home. Leaving 1905. Leaving my
Kathleen.

What would I do when I got back to my time?
I couldn't stay on Mackinac Island. Not after all I'd
experienced here. The memories would be too painful.
I couldn't go back to Kansas. There was nothing there
for me.

I walked slowly back up the hill to Skull Cave, almost hoping someone would see me, and recognize me, and take me off to jail. But no such luck.

I finally arrived at the back of the rocks, and went through the portal. I placed the covering over the hole. Then I took the stick of dynamite that I'd brought with me from 1905, and held it in my hand.

I knew this would be it. If I did this, there would be no way back, ever. I remembered that day I'd jumped from the docks into the icy waters of Lake Huron. I knew if I thought about it too long, I'd never do it. It was the right thing. I knew I just had to jump.

I lit the fuse and sat the dynamite in front of the portal, then climbed down the rocks as quickly as I could, and ran. I was quite a way down the trail when I heard the blast. And I knew I needed to get as far away from the scene of the crime as possible, before some park ranger came and arrested me.

As I walked down Fort Hill toward town, I was suddenly hit with the cold splash of reality. I couldn't simply go back to my hotel room. I didn't *have* a hotel room. I'd been gone from 1975 for nearly four months. I had just left, leaving all my clothes in my room, with no explanation to anyone. I honestly didn't think I'd ever be back.

Those at the Murphy might have thought I just left without checking out. But my car was still on the docks in St. Ignace. Julie was probably worried sick about me. Everyone probably thought that I'd drowned, or something.

And Katia. Maybe she was *glad* I was missing, after what she thought of me. But *whatever* she thought of me, I knew I had to face her, and anyone else I had to face.

It was close to midnight, and I decided that I would wait until morning to deal with everything. That would give me some time to cook up an explanation for my four-month absence. It would have to be a good one, because I would probably have to give the story to the authorities also.

I walked back up the hill, past the Governor's Mansion, and down the back way, to the bench at the top of the west bluff. I sat there, looking at the wedding cake house, wishing Kathleen would come out the front door. But she didn't. She couldn't. She lived in a different time. She was just part of the fading trail of a dying comet.

I wondered if she might still be alive. But I knew she wasn't. If she were, she would be over one hundred, and she would owe me a cookie. I was sure that she had died, just when she said she would — at eighty-eight — and that I owed her a penny. Only I'd never be able to give it to her. She was gone. I cried at the thought.

\*    \*    \*

I watched the sunrise, and sat there on the bench, thinking, until about 8 a.m., and then I walked down the hill toward the Grand. I didn't know if it was my imagination, or if it was still in bloom this late, but I could smell the Elysium that Kathleen loved so much.

As I walked past the Grand Hotel and down the hill toward town, I saw the island come to life. Carriages heading down the hill, taking people toward town. And carriages coming up the hill, taking people to the hotel. Men were in the streets, sweeping up the horse manure. Workers riding their bikes to work. Visitors out for an early morning bike ride. Just like in 1905. Everything was just like it was 70 years before. And like it would probably be a hundred years from now.

For some reason, for that moment, my sadness left, and I felt almost hopeful. That somehow, good would come out of all that had happened, and was happening, and that *would* happen.

When I walked into the front door of the Murphy, I saw Katia at the front desk. I wondered if she would even recognize me through the beard and mustache. She looked up, and at first she *didn't* recognize me. Then she began to cry.

"David!" she cried, as she ran from behind the desk and threw her arms around my neck, almost choking me. "Oh, God, I was so worried about you."

"Worried about me? I thought you hated me."

"Where have you been? You left all your stuff, and . . ." She stopped, backed up, and hit me in the chest with her palms. "We thought you were dead!"

"Katia, it's a long story, and I'll tell you all about it. But I need to get cleaned up. Do you know where my stuff is? Is it still here?"

"Yes, it's in the storage room in back. But you've got a lot of explaining to do."

"Do you have a room available?"

"You can have the same room you had, if you want. It's vacant."

"That would be great."

She walked to the desk and made a phone call, and then grabbed the keys to the room.

"Come on. I'll take you up. Your bags will be up in a little while."

She put her arm around me, and we walked up the stairs together. She was still in tears. We walked into the room, and I sat, exhausted, on the bed.

"Katia, please don't take this the wrong way, but, I didn't know you cared. I mean, I'm sorry this affected you so much. I thought . . ."

"You are a dense boy, David. I practically threw myself at you, and you . . . that's just how I feel, ok? I wear my heart on my sleeve, and I'm just being honest."

"Katia, I'm going through a lot right now. There's so much that has happened in my life."

"You don't have to explain," she said, wiping her tears with her sleeve.

"No, Katia, I *do* have to explain. I'm in love with someone. I mean, I *was* in love with someone. I mean, I still am in love."

"Please don't explain. I need to go."

She opened the door, and started to walk through it.

"And she's dead, Katia. I'm in love with her, and she's dead," I said, sobbing.

She stopped, and came back in the room, closing the door behind her.

"Oh, God, David. I'm sorry. I didn't know."

"I know she would want me to love again, but I don't know if I ever can."

I was in tears, and she was standing next to me, holding my head to her chest. She held me as I cried, and I could feel the genuineness of her concern.

"Do you understand?" I asked.

"David, I do understand. You just need some time. And I'll be here, as close or as far as you want me to be. But I really have a good feeling about us. And I hope you don't think that I throw myself at every guy I meet. I really think we have a chance, both of us, to be happy together. It's just a feeling, but I've felt it from the first moment I met you."

"I'm pretty messed up right now."

"Look, let's be friends, ok? Good friends. I'm leaving tomorrow to go back to Chicago. We could write, and maybe you could come visit at Christmas time, and meet my family. Let's just take our time, and go from there."

A knock came at the door. Katia answered it. It was a police officer.

"Mr. Andrews, you gave us a serious scare," the officer said as he took off his hat.

"Yeah, so I've heard. I'm really sorry. I hitchhiked up to Hessel, and then went over to the island that I own there, and sort of roughed it."

"Well you should let someone know before you do something like that, especially before leaving your clothes and car behind. We located a former girlfriend of yours, Julie Stewart. She told us where you were going, and we checked on your island, but we found no sign of you there. We thought you'd drowned."

I knew I had to think fast. I remembered reading about the Tahquamenon Falls in the U.P. in a travel brochure, and hoped my next lie wouldn't get me deeper into trouble.

"Well, I hitched around the U.P. for a while. I wanted to see Tahquamenon Falls, and some of the other places up there."

"You always hitchhike in an old tux?" he asked me.

Again, I had to think fast.

"Ah, I was planning to take Katia to the Grand for dinner tonight."

I glanced at Katia. She raised her eyebrows slightly, but didn't say anything.

"Well you had a lot of people worried, and cost the taxpayers a lot of money. I'll need you to come over to the station sometime today and fill out a report," the police officer said.

"Yes, sir. I will just as soon as I can. Thank you very much. Again, I'm so sorry."

"And make sure you get on the phone and let everyone know you are all right. Especially Julie and her husband. They were worried sick about you," the officer said as he walked out the door.

I thought about how worried Julie must be, when it hit me — the officer had just said Julie and *her husband*. Julie was married. I smiled inside.

Katia leaned over and kissed me on the forehead.

"Take a shower and get some rest. And for God's sake, shave! You look horrible with a beard."

She walked to the door, and turned around.

"I'm a very honest person, David. Sometimes to a fault. If we are going to be friends, you'll need to start telling the truth."

"What do you mean?"

"I'm mean, what was that bullshit you told the officer?"

"Katia, if I would have told him the truth, he'd have me thrown in a mental institution."

"Are you going to tell *me* the truth?"

"I will, someday. But I promise, you won't believe it."

"We'll see."

She started to walk out the door again.

"Oh, do you want the room on your credit card?"

I reached inside the tux jacket for my wallet, only to feel nothing. I couldn't remember the last time I'd had my wallet. Then I looked across the room at the baseboard. "What if?" I thought.

"Katia, let me call you at the desk later. I have to locate something."

"Sure. See ya around," she said as she walked out the door.

As soon as she was gone, I walked to the baseboard. The woodwork had been refinished, but I could tell the wood was original. I went to the desk drawer and took out a pair of scissors. I pried at the wood carefully. I didn't want to break the scissors, and I certainly didn't want anyone to hear me tearing up the room.

Finally, the board came loose. I held my breath, and reached back underneath the floorboards as far as my arm would reach. I felt something. It was cloth. I grabbed it with my fingertips, then got a handhold, then pulled it out. It was one of the bags of gold I'd hid there in 1905. I reached underneath the next floor joist. Another bag. And under the next. Another. I was amazed. It was still there after seventy years.

Nearly four months before, as I traveled up I-75 toward the Mackinac Bridge, I'd been listening to stock prices on the radio. And now I laughed as I pulled the bags of gold pieces out of the floor. The gold that I'd hid there in 1905, which I'd exchanged at $20 an ounce, was now worth $180 an ounce. A law that had prohibited individual citizens from owning gold, and had been in effect for almost forty-five years, had just been repealed in October of 1974.

As I sat there looking at the money, I felt encouraged. It wasn't the money. I had money in the bank, and a little more wouldn't make that much difference. One man can only spend so much money; one person only needs so much. But that wasn't the point. It wasn't the money. It was the fact that the money was still there. That something I'd done in the past had affected the future. If some physical act could affect the future, how much more a spiritual act — an act of love.

Even though they'd erected a statue of him, Father Mark had his doubts about whether or not he'd done much to change things. Because he knew that, while people had tried to preserve his memory in stone, there was something far more important that they *couldn't* preserve in stone — the love with which he'd done what he had done.

Maybe this was why the masses always seemed to miss the point. Missed the lessons that noble men and women had tried to teach. In making institutions of their names, we'd sterilized, anaesthetized, and fossilized the life right out of the lessons they'd sought to show.

But even though the masses had missed the point, it didn't change what these individuals had accomplished. If my hiding a few bags of gold could affect the future, still be here in the future, how much more could the actions . . . no, the *true love* of individuals, affect the future; leave its residual, still resonate, in the future. And for a moment I felt I knew why this was true. Because there *was* no future. Only now, fueled, magnetized, by the spiritual reality of love.

Father Mark spoke of the far-reaching effects of love. And though he didn't feel he'd affected as much as he wanted to, I wondered how things would have been, how much worse, had he not done what he'd done. And not just him, but many others like him.

I knew that he had also been affected by fossilized rituals and lifeless institutions, just like all of us had. And that none of us had made a perfect mark on history. But in the moments when he, or anyone, had aspired past the fossilized, sterilized, traditions of mankind, and manifested true love in the world, the effects of that love would reverberate for centuries — whether people tried to stone them to death, or tried to encase their memory in stone.

Like he had said — no one will remember why the statue was there, or what they wanted to remind themselves of by putting it there. And that's why it's not up to mankind to keep score. Someone, something, much greater than mankind, is keeping score.

I wondered about the other things I'd done in my past. I'd done so many things in my life *out of harmony* with love, and they had all come back to haunt me. I looked back at 1905, and felt I'd done the right thing. Maybe that was the only reason I was there. To help her. To use the gift I'd been given to free her. I felt good about that. It was true love. I didn't need to keep score. Somehow, I hoped that what I'd done there in 1905 would affect others in a wonderful way — perhaps forever.

FIFTEEN

# A Walk in the Park

It was September 11<sup>th</sup>, 1975. It felt right, leaving on a Thursday. I was leaving Mackinac Island, and I would never be back. I *couldn't* come back. Ever. It would hurt too much. It was all over. It had been paradise. But now? I would not stay on the island, trapped by my memories.

I wanted to believe in my heart that somehow, Kathleen had found happiness. And if I knew that she had, then maybe I could try to do the same, for her sake. Katia and I would see each other at Christmas time. We were friends, but that was probably all we ever would be.

I had to say one goodbye before I left, and that was to the "big guy" in Marquette Park. It didn't look anything like him, and he certainly wasn't that tall, or that old. But the presence of the statue *felt* like his presence; commanding and larger than life.

I walked to the base of the statue, and stood there thinking about all he had taught me. There was a woman there with her little boy, and I overheard her tell him that *this was the man that discovered America*. At that exact moment, a gull sitting on Father Mark's head started laughing. And I laughed with him.

I had no sooner turned to walk away from the statue, when across the park, sitting on a blanket in the sunshine, reading a book, was the most beautiful face I'd ever seen. How could it be? It was Kathleen.

I couldn't believe it. I thought that I must be hallucinating. I walked to her slowly. I savored every moment, because I knew at any moment the vision would disappear. Then she looked up from her book, and our eyes met. And for the tiniest instant, she seemed to recognize me. But then, just as quickly, she looked back down at her book.

By this time, I stood directly beside her blanket. She looked up at me again.

"I'm sorry. Do I know you?" she asked. She had such kindness in her eyes.

"Please forgive me, I'm . . . but you look so familiar to me."

"It's the picture hanging at the Murphy Hotel," she said with an understanding smile. "I get that all the time." She paused. I gave her a puzzled look. "It's my grandmother," the young beauty replied.

"The picture. Of course. That's where . . . I mean, that's where I must have . . ." I stopped short, not knowing what else to say.

"People spot the resemblance often. I'm so proud to look like her. My father told me that I have her lilt too; that I sound just like her when I talk."

"You do," I stated, before I could think about what I was saying, mesmerized by the familiar rhythm of her voice. "I mean, you must have. I could listen to it for hours."

"Do you come to the island often?" she asked.

"No, no. This is my first visit here. But I've been here all summer."

"That's strange. I don't remember seeing you this summer."

"Ah, I sort of kept to myself."

"I've lived here all my life," she offered. "Our family has been here for five generations."

"Yes, I read all about your grandfather, Paul Martin. He was a wonderful man."

"Yes, he was a wonderful man. He took very good care of my grandmother, after her first husband was killed. But Paul Martin was actually my step-grandfather. My real grandfather's name was Lovit. He was the man that my grandmother had an affair with. The man that killed . . ."

"Yes, I know. I mean, I read . . ." I cut her off. I couldn't hear any more. It was all too much for me. I saw so much of Kathleen in her. My eyes began to tear.

I know I would have looked, sounded so strange to anyone else. But in her eyes was the same understanding look that Kathleen always had.

"My name is Katie."

"My name is David Lo . . . Andrews."

I'd been using the name Lovit so long, that I'd almost forgotten it wasn't my real name. I was glad I'd caught myself in time, and very relieved that I could finally use my real name again.

"My father's name was David," she said. "You know, you resemble my father. I wonder if we are related."

"Related? Oh, no, I'm sure we're not," I replied, struggling to maintain my composure, being overwhelmed by the connections that my mind began to make.

"Your name sounds so familiar. I know I've heard it somewhere before," she said, putting her finger to her lips, and squinting, trying to remember where she'd heard it before.

"Katie, is your father still alive?"

"He died last year."

I could tell from the look on her face, that thinking about him made her happy, but sad at the same time. I understood those feelings completely.

"You miss him," I said.

"Yes, I do. *Very* much," she affirmed. "It hurts that he is gone, but I wouldn't have missed knowing him for anything."

"My father died last year also. I didn't get to know him very well. He left when I was four. I'm so glad you got to know your father."

"Thank you. That's very kind of you," she said warmly.

"And your grandmother, is she still alive?" I asked, almost certain I knew the answer.

"She died on my eighteenth birthday. August 8th, 1961. She was eighty-eight years old. And she was healthy and happy till the day she died."

I don't know if I smiled outwardly, but I was smiling within. She was happy. She was healthy. She was eighty-eight. And she had won our bet.

"Did she have any other children besides your father?"

"Oh, yes. She had two more boys, and five girls. Eight children in all."

"She always said that was her lucky number," I said aloud, and then tried to cover with, "I read that somewhere."

"Well, Mr. Andrews. From the things you know about my family history, it sounds like you've been to our local library. But there is something that I'll bet you a penny to a cookie you haven't read."

"A penny to a cookie? A penny to a cookie? I don't think a penny will buy a cookie anymore," I said as I laughed through my tears. How nice to hear such a familiar voice say those familiar words.

"Well, Miss Katie, where can I read this that I haven't read?" I asked in a tone that mocked her lilt.

"Well, Mr. Andrews. If you will be so kind to escort me to our local library, I just might have access to some of my grandmother's items, not available to the general public," she said with a smile, putting on an extra strong dash of the Irish.

As we walked to the library, talking to Katie was like talking to a long lost friend. We both felt it. Maybe she felt like she was talking to her father. I felt like I was talking to my Kathleen, and a daughter, and a granddaughter, all at the same time.

We entered the library, and Katie walked up to the librarian. I couldn't make out what was being said, but the librarian left, and then returned shortly, and handed Katie a key.

"Come with me," Katie said, as she grabbed me by the hand, and led me up the stairs to a room full of old wooden file cabinets. She walked across the room, right to the cabinet she wanted, inserted the key, and opened the drawer. Out of it, she took several books, all bound in faded fabric.

Each book was a treasure, because each page contained the days, hours, minutes, and seconds of Kathleen's precious thoughts. They were her memoirs.

I can't describe the joy I felt as we sat there in the library reading them. I cried at every page, and though anyone else might have thought it strange, Katie didn't seem to think it strange at all. And though she had read them all many times before, she took delight in every page along with me, as if she shared my joy.

With the memoirs were several letters, one of which I recognized immediately. It was my handwriting on a Grand Hotel envelope — my letter to Kathleen, telling her goodbye.

When we finished, we sat there for quite a while. Then Katie got the strangest look on her face. She got up and walked slowly back to the drawer, almost like she was in a daze. Then she walked back to the table, just as slowly, and laid a large, sealed, pouch envelope on the table. On the outside of it, in Kathleen's handwriting, was my full name. My *real* name!

I opened it, and tipped it to pour out the contents onto the table. Out fell a small envelope. On the front of it was written: *To My Dearest David.*

"Oh my God! " Katie said. "I knew your name sounded familiar. And the things that grandmother said to me. They all make sense now. It's for you, isn't it?" she said slowly, looking at me with shock and amazement, and yet with a recognition, as though she knew the secret of who I was.

"Yes, Katie, I think so."

My heart was pounding as I opened the letter and began to read.

My Dearest David,

I hope . . . no, I _know_ that someday you will read this letter. It was so out of character for me to write to you that day about being in your play. But I did it because somehow, I knew that it was meant to be. And all the good that has happened between us was meant to be. And therefore, I can't help but believe that in all this good, that you could escape the inevitability of reading this letter.

So here it is, my love. All my love to you. Thank you for loving me. Thank you for believing in me. Thank you for all the precious things you have taught me. I will never forget you. How could I? Every time I look in our precious son's eyes, I see you, my love. He even has your sense of humor — but I laugh at his jokes anyway (smile), just like I did at yours.

You have changed my life forever, and you have taught me the beauty of true love — the kind that gives, instead of takes. You have given me a rose without thorns that will never wilt or fade.

And one more thing, my love: rest your heart that I know where you came from, and I understand why you couldn't stay. I know the secret of Temporalis Fissura, and it will remain our secret. Yours, mine; the secret of the few. The secret of our love, and of our time.

Be happy, and healthy, my love, and live till at least eighty-eight (smile).

Yours, of course.
Kathleen

I tipped the pouch envelope again, to pour out its remaining contents, and out fell my wallet; the one that I had lost in 1905 — with my 1975 driver's licence, credit cards, currency, and all.

I looked at Katie, her grandmother's smile radiating back at me.

"Was it all worthwhile?" she asked, with tears in her eyes.

"Oh, yes, Katie," I said. "All of it."

\*     \*     \*

As the *Huron* backed slowly away from the dock, I looked up at that blue Mackinac sky, then at the white walls of the fort, gleaming in the sun. At the base of the fort, in the middle of the park, I saw the statue of Father Mark, standing guard over the town, over the harbor, over Mackinac Island.

The boat pulled out into the Straits, and I looked up to see that grand hotel on the hill, and then the wedding cake house on the bluff. I could almost see Kathleen standing on the bluff — smiling, waving goodbye. The whole time I could hear a symphony orchestra playing Kathleen's song in my mind.

Kathleen was one of those beautiful souls whose heart resonated with life's finest notes, its most stirring melodies, and its richest chords. The beauty of her heart still resonates in mine, while life's subtle rhythm, the rhythm of time, pulses almost subliminally, moving my life forward, away from 1905, 1975, and away from Mackinac Island. But not away from my Kathleen.

That was the summer of 1975. It was my first and last time on Mackinac Island. Her name was Kathleen, and yes, I did love her more than life itself.